I0619031

REQUIEM FOR AN
ASTRONAUT

NP Novellas:

REQUIEM FOR AN
ASTRONAUT

Daniel Bennett

NewCon Press
England

First published in the UK August 2021 by
NewCon Press
41 Wheatsheaf Road,
Alconbury Weston,
Cambs, PE28 4LF

NPN007 (limited edition hardback)
NPN008 (paperback)

10 9 8 7 6 5 4 3 2 1

Requiem For An Astronaut copyright © 2021 by Daniel Bennett

Cover Art copyright © 2021 by Ian Whates

All rights reserved, including the right to produce this book, or portions
thereof, in any form.

ISBN:

978-1-912950-90-4 (hardback)
978-1-912950-91-1 (paperback)

Cover layout and design by Ian Whates

Typesetting and editorial meddling by Ian Whates
Text layout by Ian Whates

'I was like the needle in a compass carried through the forest by an orienteer with a thumping heart.'

– Tomas Tranströmer 'Homewards'

One

I saw the smoke on the horizon, a black cord smudging the low cloud of morning. The organ farm, I realised, but turned away immediately to busy myself at the edges of the garden. The smoke drifted, diffusing in the area of sky beyond the walls. I concentrated on hoeing the thin soil, falling back on a few logical truisms to make myself feel better. *It was always going to happen. Only a matter of time.*

Occasionally, I would see the workers from the farm on the edges of my corner of the landscape, groups of young people in white scrubs. Perhaps they knew the dangers involved, with the growing presence of the Lud cults outside East City. In my experience, the young understood the risks but never understood the outcome. More than that, they didn't understand how you could *become* the outcome.

That morning, I had gone down to the bottom of the garden to check the apple tree. I moved to this outpost for many reasons – to return to my research, to appreciate the silence, to escape from people – but gradually, the apple tree had become a kind of centre for me. Two years ago, on the day I'd left East City, I passed through the Nordmarket on my way out, stopping to pick up some the necessary tech supplies for my retreat to the sticks.

Of course, I'd had another reason to be there – reasons related to Joan's appearance above the market those weeks before – and I spent most of my time taking trace recordings of the area. Besides, part of me had probably wanted to finish my time in East City with a visit to the market, as it felt like the apotheosis of life there: antic, voluble and intense, where anything might happen. Where anything had happened, the moment Joan had appeared.

That day, however, the miracle proved more prosaic. A crowd had gathered around one of vendors, who had set up a stall with a small bag of apples. Most had been unable to afford the fruit, but I bought one for myself, the skin blending from green to red, like an intricate model of colour theory. I kept that apple on the seat beside me, as I piloted my hover away from East City. Our relationship with things is always more complicated than we understand, and the apple had become a *thing* for me beyond its simple appleness: a symbol, an allegory. Maybe I related it to Joan and her visitation of the Nordmarket; maybe I related it to my past life. I kept it with me on the journey; past the waypoint station at the edge of East City, where I felt a sense of heroism in replying 'I won't be coming back' when the border guard had asked me for my return date. Along the bloated river, where the dull grey waters lapped across the flood plain. Out across the greyed-out landscape, the sea glistening in the distance like tarnished oil. And finally to the stretch of land I had arranged to occupy, going through months of agreements and waivers before I qualified to become a resident. I didn't own the land – you couldn't own the land beyond East City – but agreed a semi-permanent lease, which was all I really needed. On my first evening in my new home I ate the apple, looking out over the grey land. And once I was done I planted the pips in the ground, more as a symbolic act than with any kind of expectation. As the shoot formed into a stalk, and the stalk into a thin trunk, I'd taken this as a blessing on my decision, not to mention the endeavours I'd undertaken.

Later in the morning I stepped outside the walls of the house. I'd seen a gull some weeks ago, blown inland from the sea, or scavenging for food, and as I pottered about in the garden, I thought I'd heard a sound of its call. There was no sign of it in the sky, but I stepped out of the gate to see if it had landed. As I returned to the house, I saw the woman. She crouched on the ground behind a thin clump of pale grass, watching me, but it was almost impossible for her to hide in her white scrubs. The smoke on the horizon had drifted, blending with the air from black to grey.

'You'll get muddy there,' I called out.

After a few moments, the woman stood up, looked behind her. She wore her blondish hair in a scruffy bowl cut, and carried a grey cloth bag strapped over her chest. I could see that the soil had caked over her scrubs.

'I didn't want to scare you.'

'Young people don't scare me.' I didn't say it, but I think we both understood: *not when there are other things to scare me.*

'I meant...' If it was possible to look awkward and terrified at the same time, the poor thing managed it. 'I need a place to hide.'

'What's your name?'

'Cal.'

'Nice to meet you, Cal. I'm Bart.'

I watched as she processed that information. She adjusted her balance, moving from foot to foot.

'Are you from the organ farm, Cal?' I pointed back the way she had come, towards the column of smoke.

'I'm hungry,' she said, by way of an answer. 'And tired.'

'You can come inside. I get visitors so rarely it will be a treat for me.'

She didn't respond. I walked ahead of her, through the gateway of the walled garden, and held the door open behind me. After Cal passed through, I closed the gate, punched in the code.

'Just to be safe,' I said.

Inside the house I directed Cal to remove her boots and bag, and set about preparing food in the protein printer. The centrifuge whirred, the faux meat crystallising into filaments, those filaments into fibres, and those fibres into sinew, pinkish and grey, like an odd form of dirty snow.

'You're not worried,' she said. 'About the cult?'

'They leave me to myself.'

In truth, I'd only seen scant evidence of the cult over the last year, a band of its members passing towards their site in one of the ruined towns to the north. You recognised them by their badges (a symbol of a circle and three lines with a slash through them, like an erased skull) their renegade manner, their slightly dazed expressions. I picked up the extent of their rampages from the rare occasions I tuned into meme chats and the holotube, but I'd renounced my implants since leaving the city, and the news travelled slowly. I went through the routine of my life, aware of the excesses of the various cults, and making sure I didn't provoke them with anything obvious. I had been careful about that. At night, I locked the doors, always understanding that every lock could be broken, every door smashed down.

How else to live in these days?

Cal moved to the window, looking out over the walled garden. 'Is that a tree?'

'I grew it myself.' The pride in my voice surprised me. I realised that Cal was my first visitor in the house.

'Can I see it?'

'Eat first. Rest up. You've had a difficult night, I think.'

She nodded, absently, almost abstractly. Lost in memories of whatever had occurred, maybe. My words seemed to act as permission to give into whatever pent up feeling had brought her here. She looked, suddenly, exhausted. She sat down at the small table dividing the kitchen from the living area, supporting her head in her hands as I busied myself with the food. I brewed her a cup of tea, and served it with the faux meat smothered in a savoury vitamin gravy. She ate from the plate rapaciously, with an almost animal energy.

'It's good,' she said, when she saw me watching. She didn't bother to swallow before she spoke.

'It's passable,' I said, although it gave me an odd feeling of warmth to feed her. Long lost moments of familial intimacy with my daughter returned: a different time, a different life.

'Back at the farm, our protein printer never worked properly,' Cal said. 'The meat was sloppy. Just this horrible meaty gloop.' The playfulness of her words made her smile, but almost immediately another expression rinsed through her features. Sadness, perhaps, or survivor's guilt.

'If you want to talk about what happened, that's fine.'

She shook her head. She picked over the remnants of her food, making sure to spoon up the last of the vitamin gravy. Finally, she pushed the plate away, belching softly.

'Do you have somewhere I can sleep?'

We walked up the short flight of stairs to the mezzanine. The building had been constructed out of raw concrete in little more than an afternoon, an East City contractor who had flown his construction unit out here, warning me all the time about my liability for any attacks. I had designed the property myself, based on a photograph I had seen in a museum of an old style of building. The museum exhibition had described it as an oasthouse, used to dry hops in an early form of industrialised brewing. The conical roof had always attracted me, but the wall that wrapped around the high garden wall was my own embellishment: a little fort to hide out in, and protect me from the demands of the world.

I showed Cal the bedroom, and the annex with the toilet area and the shower, the water processed from the sea in a desalination unit. 'You should take those clothes off.'

She shot me a look, almost like betrayal. 'I'm trusting you now,' she said. 'I'm putting myself in your care.'

I laughed. 'I'm an old man.'

'I want you to understand. I can defend myself.' She had brought the cloth bag up the stairs, and I saw her fumble towards it. I wondered what weapons she had in there. A knife, maybe? I doubted that Cal would have had access to a bolt gun. It occurred to me that I had let a stranger in my home.

'I'm sure you can. But I'm an old man,' I repeated. 'And I really mean you no harm. But you'll feel better if you take off those muddy clothes. I have a robe you can wear.'

She held my gaze for a moment. Such an odd young woman; an ingrained seriousness, almost like something hardwired. A switch seemed to flip, and she evidently decided I was as benign as I claimed. Without any display of modesty, she began pulling off the scrubs. The humid scent of her body became unavoidable, and I wondered if I was as old as I claimed.

I spent the rest of the morning in the lab, going through old data models, synthesising the outputs with recent readings I'd taken over the last weeks, looking for anomaly patterns in some of the radiation traces. The conical roof of the building held most of the scanning equipment, utility hidden inside its form. My access to data sets came from open sources, and some old friendships I maintained in certain research centres across the world. My career had not been distinguished, but it had been dogged, and I still benefitted from working on the early stages of the space programme, back when we first found ways of adapting the technology from the White Ship. I decided early on that I would have to keep my work hidden, although I'd originally been aiming to hide myself from government and the space agency, not from the Lud cult.

I walked quietly to the mezzanine from time to time and checked on my guest. Cal slept heavily, curled up tightly in my robe at the furthest edge of the bed. I would need to make a bed up for the night on the sofa in the lounge, as it looked unlikely she would be ready to leave any time soon. Again, it surprised me how quickly I had adjusted to this surprise visitor, how ready I had been to absorb her presence into my routine. My thoughts naturally turned to my daughter, Karla. When I'd told her of my plans to quit the city she'd been furious, and I hadn't quite escaped a sense of guilt. I'd been a distant father, and an abysmal husband to her mother who had died many years ago. My relocation outside the city had caused Karla's feelings of abandonment to resurface, and the last time she'd left a message for me on my voice chat had been filled with recriminations. 'You'll understand if I take it personally that you've decided to spend your last years away from me and from your grandchildren.'

By the time Cal came downstairs it was late afternoon, and I was sitting outside, treating myself to a small cup of coffee, synthetic of course, but a pretty good approximation. I had some real coffee hidden away somewhere in the house, although I planned on saving that for a greater occasion than my refugee from the organ farm.

'I'm sorry. I must have been asleep for hours.' She stepped down into the garden, playing a hand through her hair. The robe had parted around the belt, but just about covered her body. She must have noticed my gaze, because she adjusted the material around her, not entirely banishing an air of immodesty, which I guessed that came from her life in the organ farm. I gestured to the empty seat beside me, but she shook her head.

'I hope you're feeling better.'

'I am. Thank you.' She paused, looking out over the garden. 'I should get ready to leave.'

I laughed at the hesitancy in her voice. 'It doesn't make much sense for you to leave now.'

'Why?'

'Where would you go?'

'I'm heading to East City. I have a sister there. Elsa.'

'East City is a long way away, Cal. Can Elsa come and collect you?'

She shook her head. 'I haven't seen her in a year or so. I'm not even sure…' Her voice trailed off.

11

'That she'd want to come to collect you?'

'No. That she's even still there. She's working for a subsidiary of the organ farm I haven't heard from her for a while.' She seemed to be holding something back, but I had no desire to probe her relationship with her family.

'Well, without some kind of transport, then I'm afraid you're not going to get very far. It would take days to walk. Maybe weeks.'

'Can you take me there?'

'I hadn't planned on returning to East City for some time.'

'But you have a hover?'

I pointed to the bottom of the garden. 'I keep it under cover down there. I haven't used it since I first moved here. But if you're thinking of stealing it, the security protocols are linked to my ID.'

I'd meant the jibe about stealing the craft as a joke, but Cal looked wounded, even betrayed. 'I would never take it from you. Ever.'

'I know that. I'm sorry.'

To make amends, I went back into the house and fixed her a cup of the tea. By the time I returned, she was standing by the apple tree. Still only a sapling, it barely reached Cal's shoulder. I was struck by the similarity between these two forms of life, prospering in the uncertain surroundings.

'It's amazing that you've managed to grow it,' Cal said as I approached. 'All of the garden is amazing.'

She was being generous, but I thanked her anyway. I'd managed to cultivate some lichen and moss on the concrete of the wall, and in one area I was experimenting with fungus and mushrooms. I'd created a small rockery where I hoped to encourage some small succulents to develop. 'I'd like to take some credit for the tree. But I threw the pips away, and it took care of itself.'

'We tried growing so many things in the farm, but none of them took.'

'The soil is too acidic,' I replied, aware I sounded like some kind of ancient homesteader.

Cal reached out and pushed at the thin trunk, smiling as the tree sprang back as she pushed at it. 'It's such a beautiful thing. Will it grow fruit?'

'Maybe, one day. Though I imagine they'll be too sharp to eat.'

She frowned. 'That's disappointing.'

'I've been thinking,' I said. 'Why don't you stay here tonight, and we can both go over to the farm tomorrow. There may be some kind of transport we can salvage, to get you on your way.'

I'd expected some kind of reaction, an expression of fear about what lay back at the farm, but Cal continued to focus on the tree, teasing at it with her fingers, as though strumming an instrument.

'Do you think they've gone?'

'The cult? I don't know. But we can keep our distance. My feeling is they tend to move on after one of these raids.'

'A few of them started working in the farm a month before. They infiltrated us.'

'Still, I doubt they'll be using it as a base. Did you have security?'

She nodded. 'One of the firms established a unit with us. ExCorp. But they were hopeless. Most of them fled when the raiders came. The rest were killed. I saw them killed.'

It was the first time she'd talked about what had happened, and I could see the memory had shaken her. She walked away from the tree and sat down at the table, reaching for the cup of tea. I left it a moment before I joined her.

'I don't think we need to worry too much. I know the terrain, and we can travel in the evening, when we'll be less noticeable.'

'Maybe you're right. It might be my only way out of here.'

Whether it was fair or not, I felt that there was an implicit request in her words, as though she wanted me to intercede, uncover the hover and fly her back to East City. It would be difficult to explain my reluctance in agreeing to this, so I decided not to acknowledge it at all.

'Do you know what happened to the transports at the organ farm?'

Cal shook her head. 'Mother Ray kept a couple of hovers in a garage out the back. But we weren't allowed to use them.'

'Who is Mother Ray?'

'She ran the farm. We all called her that.' She coloured slightly, as though embarrassed.

'Do you know what happened to her?'

Cal shook her head. 'I hadn't seen her that day. Not since the confusion the previous night.'

'What happened the previous night?'

'We all saw Saint Joan.'

I had never liked that name. I would never like that name, because it stood against everything I believed, everything I wanted for Joan and her memory. But I couldn't help myself. I reached out and grabbed Cal's arm. 'What did you say?'

She pulled her arm away from me. She looked wounded, even scared. 'Saint Joan. We saw her appear, about a week before the attack. What's wrong?'

'Tell me what happened,' I said. 'You need to describe everything you saw.'

Two

That evening a skud made its way across the sky, flying low from the port along the coast. Cal and I were approaching the organ farm under the cover of darkness as it came over us. The skud moved slowly, cruising on its gravity jets before reaching the necessary height to engage the drive. It moved like something primordial, a vast beast from a distant prehistoric age, its structure redefining the night sky. It had often occurred to me that the space authority routed the flight paths from East City out across this area as a provocation to the cults. Perhaps I'd spent too long in looking for hidden meanings and designs in phenomena that were, by nature, totally arbitrary. Others might have experienced a sense of pride in witnessing such a validation of a life's work, but I felt no sense of responsibility as I watched the skud, any more than I would have done if someone had cut down my apple tree to make a bow.

Cal stood by my side, watching the skud pass. We could make out the lights from the bridge, the shadows that might have been the figures of the crew, saying goodbye to home before heading out to the beyond. The sound of the drive filled the silence; the lights from the craft cast a soft glow against Cal's features. She looked almost awestruck, amazed. I remembered the times in my life when I had witnessed the first test flights, the sense of hope we experienced during those times, as we tried to adapt the alien technology from The White Ship into our human designs. As I watched the skud now, I searched for those lost feelings, like an amputee reaching towards a phantom limb. The craft altered its course, rising into the atmosphere, the thrusters burning its passage. We continued walking, and a few moments later I made out the bright bluish light of its drive initiating, blasting the ship outwards through space.

We'd left the house as the sun began to go down. Cal walked ahead of me, suddenly anxious to reach the organ farm, impatient with the pace I was keeping along the uneven ground. I had brought a staff with me, a cane of a dense plastic which I used whenever walking beyond the immediate area around the house. The ground was spongy and wet, the water table rising from the encroaching seawater. Under the light of the stars, the ground had an unreal texture and colour to it, glistening with a molluscan featurelessness. I'd also brought a pack of equipment, to take readings from the area.

Earlier, as Cal and I had sat together in the garden, we talked about Joan's appearance. Cal had been guarded and reserved, still unnerved by my reaction to what she'd told me. I'd done my best to apologise but one thing I had learned about Cal during our short time together was that her responses offered little room for compromise. She had returned to the defensive young woman in the bedroom, who had acted so betrayed when she thought that I'd been threatening her. At one stage I thought she might pack up and leave.

'It happened at night,' she told me eventually. 'The farm workers were divided into two shifts, day and night. We all ate together at the same time, breakfast for one group, dinner for another, although the meals were usually the same printed gloop. But Mother Ray always liked us to eat together. She said it was important.

'I'd heard the stories about Saint Joan from other people, but I didn't believe them. Or I thought they were exaggerated. Someone had once shown me one of the clips, but I assumed it was a fake. It looked like a fake. It even looked like a fake when it actually happened, and she appeared floating in the space above the farm.'

'How high was she?'

Cal shrugged. 'Twice the height of this house. We could see her through one of the domes. But she moved down towards the ground. People began to panic, and ran from the building.'

The description tallied with the appearances throughout East City, particularly the occasion at the Nordmarket. Although I couldn't really condone the superstitions which had grown up around Joan, it was easy to understand how they might have occurred. Myth and fable occupy the vacuum outside of reason, and up until this time no scientist had been able to describe why Joan had started appearing in this way. Not through lack of trying.

'Did she speak?'

Cal shook her head. 'She looked as if she might have been talking. As though she was having a conversation with someone we couldn't see. I heard someone say that she spoke at the Nordmarket, but we couldn't hear anything. It was like an excerpt from a holo, a transmission gone wrong. Lots of distortion, like a colour field.' She paused. 'Do you believe what people say?'

'What's that?'

'That she's a warning, an omen.'

'That's what the cults would like you to believe. It adds credence to their insane view of the world.'

'But only the next day the cult stormed the building.'

I laughed. 'That's a specious argument, Cal. You said your group had been infiltrated by Luds. All it would take is for them to be whipped into a frenzy by Joan's appearance. That doesn't mean Joan caused the massacre, or even warned of it. At the most, it means that those responsible used her appearance as an excuse.'

Cal said nothing, weighing what I'd said with a slight movement of her head.

'Anyway,' I continued. 'It's not the first time she's appeared around here.'

'How do you know that?'

17

'It's why I moved out here.' I paused. 'It's the area that's had the most sightings. Skud pilots started seeing her on the flight paths from East City. It's something to do with the trace patterns of the warp field. We don't really know how many sightings there have been.

'Why is that important to you?'

'I knew Joan. I worked with her, years before. We were friends. I'm trying to understand what happened, how we might have stopped it. I don't fool myself that we'll ever get Joan back.'

It was the first time I had voiced this sentiment, and my voice caught as I spoke. Did I really believe it? Or rather, would I have done all I had done if I really did believe it? Probably not. I'd dedicated what remained of my life to finding a trace of Joan. Would I have done that if the quest had been hopeless?

Cal took a moment to process everything I had told her. If anyone could be said to think visibly, then Cal was such a person. She sat, playing her fingers through a lock of her hair, her eyes staring off into space. She was a serious young woman, whom I guessed had been this way long before the events that had led her to my door.

'We should head over to the organ farm tonight.' She glanced up at me. 'Will you still come with me?'

Up until this point, I don't think I'd really been prepared for what we might find at the organ farm. I knew that the cults had a reputation for violence and ruthlessness, but that was only ever an abstract to me, and I hadn't witnessed any of it for myself. Any life in East City is never far from violence, but I had been fortunate to live a largely sheltered existence, although some of the experimental work involving the early days of space travel had led me to witness things that anyone would rather forget.

The organ farms drew young people like Cal by offering decent wages and accommodation, when those things were often in short supply. Needing the kind of space for operations that was at a premium in the cities, the farms spread out in the surrounding areas, sometimes occupying the ruins of the declining towns or old sites of habitation. Some of the companies involved (because these were private enterprises, and not the collectives they tried to appear) propagated the image of campus life. You know the kind of thing: a chance for the young to be young; a meeting of minds and freedom for the curious. In many ways, it had been what snared me in the space programme, that campus where I'd spent the significant part of my life and career. In reality, the work in the organ farms was intensive, a sweatshop more than a scientific park, and the only thing that separated it from exploitation was the opportunity (I imagined) for low level dopamine fixes and bed hopping. The one close to me had even occupied the site of a rundown school, although using the ground more than the building for its spread of incubation chambers and culture plants.

By the time we reached the edge of the farm complex, everything that had happened became grimly obvious. A young woman lay face down by a gate at the edge of the property. She was around the same age as Cal and, like Cal, she wore white scrubs. Her back had been singed by a bolt-gun blast, and it looked as though she'd been hacked at with blades. This first display of the carnage made me pause, not really out of fear but more from a sense of shock at the sheer violence on display. Cal froze at the sight of her.

I touched her arm. 'Do you want to go on?'

'This is Mae. We sat together every day for breakfast. She was running behind me as I left.'

'Cal, I know this is upsetting. We either move on or head back now. We can't risk being outside for too long.'

'I don't want to head back.'

'Then how do we get in?'

She pointed in a vague direction beyond the largest of the bubble domes. I managed to pull her away, although she kept glancing back at the fallen woman.

'Do you think she died with a shot aimed at me?'

'I'm not sure it does any good thinking like that. She's dead. Just be grateful you're alive.'

We crossed the forecourt towards the entrance. We passed more bodies along the way: a young man with his hands hacked off and a bolt gun blast to the head, a group of corpses that had been set on fire. I reached out for Cal's arm, and pulled her along with me. We made our way into the interior of the building through a chute entrance leading into the largest of the bubble domes. The organ farm had been erected quickly around the existing structure of the school, a tangle of builds and bubble domes bolted onto the remains. Cal had told me that transport was housed in a garage at the back of the complex, but we agreed to make our way through the interior to avoid being too exposed.

The years of disease had given rise to the organ farms. In part, this was a consequence of the early years of space travel, in part the slide in the environment. Our reach towards space was already under way by the time the White Ship arrived, with the new viruses and bacteria brought to Earth from Mars by colonists, when they returned with their booty of ore and minerals. For fifty years or so the world reeled from outbreaks of diseases, some of them localised and easily controlled, others more virulent and aggressive. One recent outbreak had been of bacteria that attacked the vitreous body of the eyeball, essentially rotting the eyes from the inside out. Organ farms had developed to supply the shortfall for transplants, growing the gene edited tissue in culture tanks. These replacement organs were short lived, but that only made the endeavour a profitable business.

The culture tanks fanned out in rows, leading from the central control point. Amongst the dead I saw figures in black uniforms with a red logo of ExCorp, one or two of them still armed: members of the private security firm who protected the plant. They looked hardly older than the farm workers, little more than children employed to face dangers they hadn't understood.

Cal walked ahead of me, into the bubble dome.

'Was it here?' I asked. 'Where you saw Joan?'

'That's right.' She pointed above us. 'She appeared in the sky and drifted down through the bubble.'

'She came through the dome?'

Theoretically, I knew that Joan would have no corporeal form, although I wasn't sure that this had ever been proven empirically. It represented significant data. I retrieved the instruments from my bag, the scanner I had modulated with some of the particle data from the returning skuds after they engaged their drives, along with a medical console which contained Joan's genetic profile. I'd accompanied Cal to help her return to East City, and my visit here had concerns beyond my loyalty to Joan. Still, I couldn't help but spend several minutes pacing the room, taking readings and looking for environmental fluctuations beyond the control level. Maybe it was longer. I have always found work to be a necessary distraction from the world around me. Sooner or later, I realised that Cal had disappeared from my side. Not long after, I was walking deeper through the corridors, hissing out her name.

She spoke clearly, loudly, her voice sharp and sudden in the silence of the dead farm. 'I'm here!'

I found her in a large dormitory, where the beds had been overturned and scorch marks from bolt weapons marked the walls. As I stepped into the room I saw a pile of bodies that had been pushed against the furthest point of the dorm and loosely covered with bedsheets, although I doubted Cal had done this. Perhaps there had been other survivors, or more squeamish members of the cult had sought to hide their crimes. The air stank of the coppery tang of blood, and the pervasive acridity of burnt hair and skin. You could almost taste it.

Cal sat on her knees, picking through an upturned metal cabinet beside one of the beds. She gathered together: a small book, an old-style picture frame containing an image I couldn't see, a soft toy of a frog.

'What are you doing?' I tried to keep the irritation out of my voice.

'This was my bed. These are my things.'

'Well, gather them up quickly. We need to move.'

She looked up at me. For a moment she looked far younger than I thought her to be, and when she spoke I was returned to countless conversations with my daughter, where the demands of adulthood had intruded on the world of a child. 'You've been spending time on what you want to do. I want to gather my belongings.'

'I'm sorry. I got caught up in something.'

'I know you only came with me because I mentioned Saint Joan. I'm not stupid.'

'That wasn't the only reason. I came to help you.'

'So that you won't feel responsible for me.'

'That's not it at all. I don't think we should be having this conversation now. For all we know, we may have been seen on our way over here.'

'You don't understand. This was my home.'

'We'll get you back to your sister…'

She spoke sharply. 'Elsa's gone. I don't know how I'll be able to find her. This was my home. This is where I belonged.' She looked up at me. 'Our parents are dead. We were homeless in East City. The organ farm was our chance to escape all of that. I don't know what to do.'

Her expression had been so plaintive and confused I hadn't known what to say.

A noise reverberating from outside in the corridor, a sudden clattering, took away my chance to speak. Cal and I exchanged glances, although neither of us made a sound. As Cal got to her feet, I walked quickly towards the wall beside the door. Cal appeared at my side.

She hissed at me, her voice an urgent whisper. 'What was that?'

'I'm not sure.'

'What should we do?'

I didn't answer. I felt suddenly too old to be crawling through the ruins of a building, hiding out from those who had inflicted a massacre. What had I been thinking?

The clattering sounded again, followed by the sharp shattering sound of broken glass. I felt the weight of the cane in my hand. It made a useless weapon, but it was all that I had.

'Someone's there,' I said. 'How do we get to the garage?'

Cal pointed further down the corridor, beyond where we had already come.

'Then we go. As quickly as possible. And then we try to get away.'

As we stepped out into the dark corridor, I saw a flash of white, and I pushed Cal away, back into the room. The figure lurched at me out of the darkness, sprawling into me. At first, I thought I was being attacked, but before I could lift the cane to defend myself, the figure turned to a dead weight and slumped against me, falling to the floor. A man, a young man, lay at my feet, bleeding from his side.

'Nathan?' Cal appeared at my side. 'I know him. He worked with me.'

The man was in his mid-twenties. Flat features and a chin strap-beard. A cognitive implant fixed into the side of his head, another implant studded in his arm. Even if the slaughter hadn't been so indiscriminate, this man would have been a natural target for the cults. He struggled to open his eyes; by the half-light of the corridor, I could see the eyeballs rolling in their sockets. Eventually, he managed to focus on Cal's face.

'Cal. It's you.'

He'd been shot in the side. The blood soaked through his scrubs in an ugly black stain. His skin had turned a greyish colour, and sweat had soaked through his hair. His breathing was shallow and pained. I could tell he was fatally wounded, and wondered how he had survived this long.

Cal bent to his side and put her hand to his face. 'What happened, Nathan?'

'I hid in one of the lockers. Someone must have heard me. They shot through the door. They didn't come back for me, and I just stayed in there, hiding. I must have passed out. I heard your voice. I could hear you both moving around. You didn't sound… like them. I thought we were being rescued.' He looked around. 'Have you found anyone else?'

Cal glanced up at me before shaking her head. 'No. No one. Did you see what happened to Mother Ray?'

The question surprised me. I wondered if we had both been keeping our designs from one another.

'The cult must have taken her,' Nathan said. He glanced down at himself, and seemed to realise that he had been badly injured. 'Look at me. Look at what they did. Cal, what am I going to do?'

His back arched in pain, and he flailed out. Cal grabbed for his hand and held it. I noticed her strength, the lithe muscles tensing in her arms.

'It's my liver, I think.' The boy gritted his teeth as he spoke. 'Can we run a new one? In one of the culture tanks. We have my gene map on file. Everything should work.'

'It would take too long, I don't…'

'It would work, Cal. I know it would work. You can put me in a coma in the med unit.'

'Nathan, I wouldn't know what to do.'

'I've had some training with med units,' I said. 'But we'd need to cultivate an organ to match his gene map. Can that be done?'

He began to cry. I knew he was too far gone to treat. We all knew it. You could see in his eyes that he'd gone too far. We waited with him while he died. He slipped away quickly, bleeding out while Cal held his hand. He stopped crying at the end. It was almost peaceful. He closed his eyes, leaned his forehead against Cal's hand as she stroked him. A faint shiver, and he was gone.

Cal stood up. She had blood on her scrubs.

'Why did we come here?'

'We came to try and find you transport back to East City.' My patience had begun to wear thin. 'I'm trying to help you, to get you where you want to go.'

'It's horrible. Horrible, *horrible.*'

'Cal, we need to keep moving. We don't know if the cult will return.'

I managed to pull her along, heading towards the back of the building. By the time we reached the outside of the garage, I knew that there was no point. The doors had been forced open, and the control mechanisms destroyed. The small hover inside had been shot to pieces, the engine broken up. The other had presumably been stolen. The rear door had been left open. Another one of the security guards lay dead not far from the exit, stretched out in the dirt. We passed the body in silence, leaving the organ farm behind, moving quickly through the darkened landscape.

Three

Cal and I hardly spoke when we returned to the house. I offered her my bed, but she set up a blanket on the floor. She lay down and curled up against the sliding door to the garden, her hand pressed against the glass. I imagined she was looking out at the apple tree, but as I climbed the stairs I saw that her eyes were closed, and heard her snoring faintly.

I envied her ability to shut down. The young man, Nathan, dying at my feet. The bodies piled up in the dormitory, covered carelessly with bed sheets. The sheer devastation that had lain in front of us as we made our way through the deserted building: casual, arbitrary, cold. I lay in bed, thinking of everything I had seen, the proximity of death in the dark, a skull grinning under soft neon. Death as a presence, controlling and rapacious, a personality with the bony hand. Superstitions on our mortality were never far from our lives. I'll admit: there in the half-light I felt scared.

I'd grown accustomed to thinking of these as my last days. Of course, I could spin life out for a while, perhaps aided by organs from a farm such as the one we had just visited – a liver or a heart plucked like rare fruit from a tree – but essentially I had moved to this house to see out my days on this Earth, and I believed in no other. I slept little, and part of the convenience – if that was the word – of the way I lived was the ability to return to my work whenever sleep eluded me. Not tonight, though. I couldn't imagine making calculations of n-space, running models of drive signatures and the impact of thrust technologies on organic matter, and the correlative action of the genome on the time signatures, the brush of particles against one another at a subatomic level. I lay in bed, and I thought of Joan.

The first time I met Joan Kaminsky, I had been part of a debriefing panel on the space agency campus in East City, examining her reactions to the first of the drive simulations on the space station orbiting Earth. Joan wore the pale-grey flight suit that was standard for a trainee in those days, although she had tied up her tight curly hair into an orange headscarf, like a chimney shaping a cloud. She stepped off the shuttlecraft only hours before, and had gone through the various decontamination protocols. Understandably, she was tired and a little distracted.

'Most of all, I feel frazzled,' she said at one point. 'I never knew what that word really meant before this moment.'

The people I worked with were serious, intelligent, utterly lacking in humour. 'Define that for us,' one of them said.

'I'm picturing it like the combination of fried and dazzled. As if I'm an egg being cooked by a white dwarf.'

I'd been the only one who had laughed at the joke, and I remember Joan catching my eye. We bonded from that first moment.

I'll admit: from that first meeting I assumed she would be too old to succeed. A wiry woman, with wiry hair and an angular face, she must have been in her late thirties when she arrived, but she possessed a graceful, purposeful muscularity, like a gymnast or a ballet dancer. In fact, in her life before the space programme she had worked as a sculptor, of all things. Over the next hours of the debrief, Joan received the various questions with a sense of patience, although (I thought at the time) an air of recently – discovered superiority. We were used to our astronauts behaving like rarer forms of life. Mostly, this manifested as arrogance, although that was missing from Joan's personality. Perhaps I'm intimating that even at this early stage she already seemed like a saint.

'Do I feel different?' she replied to one question. 'I've just encountered a new form of space. Would you expect me to feel the same?'

Over the years, I've spent many hours caught in a feedback loop of memories about Joan Kaminsky, but it's the early days that often characterise my impressions of her. The first time she entered the drive simulator. Her delight when receiving the results of her aptitude tests for navigation. Days talking around the lake on campus. Much of my time in the space programme has faded over the years, age bringing a maddening sense of incompleteness about the specifics, but with Joan there must be a sense of emotional bonding to memories, because I have almost perfect recall of my time with her. Facts: you can get rid of facts quite easily. I've spent my life trying to retrieve facts that I've lost. Feelings, though. Those are hard to erase, however much we might try.

I had found myself in the room with Joan as the result of a series of events that chimed against one another with a sense of harmony. I had only recently finished my research degree in biophysics when the White Ship descended on East City. The strange visitation of the tall white craft that had hung over the Earth for what seemed like years, but had actually been a matter of weeks; as humanity found itself kicked into a new dawn, so I found myself coming of age. My work had focussed on the integrity of cell structures at faster than light speed, a theoretical model that, with the appearance of the White Ship, led me from something arcane and recondite into essentially becoming a mechanic.

I had accepted a position in the space programme, which aimed to wrestle space travel back from the frontier capitalists, and implemented the White Ship's technology into something worthy and noble, capable of inspiring a new generation into hope and a sense of purpose. I believed – still believe, in my own slightly worn out way – in the ideals of the programme, even if they were quickly renounced. And we held to those ideals in that campus, although like all ideals they would be betrayed, because one thing that humanity has never and will never renounce is the influence of commerce and trade. Everyone in that room was being paid, after all. And someone had to pick up the tab. We only found out what the cost would be far, far later.

In the end, our main discovery regarding the new age of space travel proved to be as much human as technological. The reverse engineering of the systems discovered beneath the White Ship's berth were more straightforward than we could have hoped. Simulations showed the potential for faster-than-light travel through the bending of space. The various probes and test ships, from the smaller missile-like constructions fired out from the atmosphere to the first of the skuds, showed that our science could adapt. The issue, however, proved to be one of control inside the region the craft passed through once space was bent, which became known as n-space. Previously space exploration had evolved from the military into administrations of nation states, and from there into the new dawn of corporate space programmes, with their doomed colonies and the intricacies of space law. One thing remained constant: the pool of talent from which we drew those who piloted the craft.

I met many of those men and women in those early days of the space programme, and they were impressive achievers, as fluent in maths and physics as they were with their skills of coordination and problem solving, whose mental attitudes and sheer force of will could have wrestled a chance of life from a supernova. They were the peak of us, so who could have expected that they would have been redundant?

The mistake we made was that we expected a sense of linearity from the n-space. One of the physicists I worked with explained it quite simply. The drive allowed you to fold two sections of space and push a pin through it. The ship travelled through the pin hole. Only instead of picturing a hole, imagine an ocean with every single temporal incarnation of its mass standing side by side into infinity. The directional focus needed an element of control we couldn't really teach. Once you had the skud in an upper atmosphere, a pilot, in the sense of how we'd previously understood the role, became pretty much unnecessary. To navigate the craft through the drive path was a creative act, dependent on a sense of mental dexterity, a kind of creative visualisation of a point in space. We had nothing like that amongst the graduates of the existing waves of space programmes.

And so, we opened up our doors.

Joan Kaminsky was one of the first astronauts of the new space. Astronauts. The title seemed so ridiculous compared to its previous incarnation, as though we were hiring scrimshaw weavers or actuaries. I found a role in the team which would evaluate the effects of the drives on the human participants. None of us were medics, but we conducted analysis of the integrity of the body's systems after exposure to the drive. I would regularly be required to sit in on the evaluation interviews with the astronauts coming back from a leap through n-space. My work could have been handled remotely, but our section head, a French woman named Georgette Marnac, had other ideas. 'We are analysing people, not phenomena,' Georgette would often remind us. 'I don't want the data to get in the way of their humanity. Once we lose sight of that, we lose sight of our purpose here.' It had been good advice, although in Joan Kaminsky's case it only proved that people could become phenomena.

The recruitment programme became famous for the breadth of its reach. How to find an ideal candidate when you have no idea of who you might need? I never found out who interviewed the applicants for the space programme, or what kind of evaluation exercises had needed to be implemented, although I understood the recruitment process to be exhaustive and exhausting for those on both sides of it. In the early days, that was partly because we didn't know what we were looking for, only what we wanted to avoid. Some said that strategically minded administrators in the space programme sought to simplify the process by breeding from those accepted, creating a strand of the population with a genetic predilection for navigating space, but whether those ideas had been condoned and implemented, I couldn't say.

Whether people or phenomena, our astronauts became rarefied creatures, partly merchandise, partly gods. We probed them, questioned them, looked for signs of the effects of n-space in their blood, their tears, their shit. Sometimes, we ended up probing their remains, or what remained of their minds if they returned to us whole. It was inevitable that dubious practices became associated with the space programme. Even the greatest of our endeavours has shadows in the wings; we are all the products of dark histories. I had heard rumours of surviving astronauts being quietly dumped into secret institutions where they lived out their lives in a state of delusion. It became clear that either mentally or physically, the astronauts had left pieces of themselves behind in n-space, or allowed n-space to become a part of themselves.

I asked Joan about this once. We would meet for lunch on the campus, sometimes in the bright and airy cafeteria looking over the waterfront, or, more often, down in the sculpted park where a leading data firm had installed hologrammatic sculptures.

'You don't strike me as embracing death,' I'd said, when the conversation turned to the subject of risk.

'Of course I think about it. Not being. Shutting down.'

'There's more to it than that. Believe me.'

I hadn't wanted to tell her about some of the things I'd seen from test flights that had gone wrong. In the best cases, whole bodies were returned to us. Sometimes it became difficult to separate the astronauts from the craft, or from each other.

Joan guessed what I'd been intimating. 'Well, don't tell me too much about it. I might change my mind. I'm not a thrill-seeker, if that's what you mean.'

'Why do it?'

'People in art talk about taking risks, when really they do no such thing, unless they're producing work under repressive regimes. And we've reached the stage where most governments care little for art, because they know that it's easily co-opted into something transactional. Look at these.' She pointed at the holograms in the park, shimmering through the daylight with their pointless exuberance. 'Maybe these were once original. Maybe they represent someone's vision. But it's been duplicated, replicated out of existence. As soon as you buy something, perhaps as soon as you present the work, the work is dead.'

'It sounds like you've had a crisis of faith.'

'I wouldn't call it faith, but I've certainly had a crisis. Maybe in my own abilities, in my choices.'

'Is that why you joined us?'

She shrugged. 'I liked the idea of being part of a collective again. My early years, I dropped out of the work programme and lived in one of the abandoned areas of East City, the old avian flu district. A lot of us lived there. We had a sense of competition and shared inspiration. One person's work would drive the rest of us onwards. I made my best pieces in those days and became myself, if you know what I mean.'

'If you really needed other people, I doubt you'd have applied with us. Being a navigator on the skud is probably the loneliest job you can imagine.'

She thought about the point seriously before answering. 'I don't mean that I need people, no. But I've missed the opportunity to have my individualism define other people. There's a difference.'

I could tell she'd thought deeply on the subject. The sense of serious dedication was probably one of the reasons she'd been a successful applicant.

'People tend to think of the imagination as being a discrete, personal space,' Joan went on. 'Unknowable, really; unreachable. But that limits its power. When I heard about the recruitment drive, I realised that it offered the potential for the imagination that was far beyond anything I'd been involved with in the past. To envisage space, to control the physical world, or at least the part of it around me, through my imagination. Isn't that a creative act?'

Not long after that discussion, Joan had been piloting a light experimental skud through n-space, on a short hop jump to the edge of the solar system. Her craft materialised by the Pluto waystation, drifting and unresponsive. The majority of the crew were dead, fused to the hull of the ship. Joan had disappeared. That was thirty years ago. The first of the sightings came twenty years later: on the banks of Rivertown.

Those of us who knew something about the space programme understood the significance of that area: it was the site of the institution which housed some of the surviving astronauts. Could Joan have been tuning into old colleagues, tracing the patterns of those who understood what might have happened?

Who knew how many times Joan had appeared without being seen? Gradually, more visitations occurred. Above the Nordmarket, near the gate station to the east of East City. Finally, skud pilots began to report sightings on the flight paths above the badlands. The phenomena seemed to be linked to the drive traces from the skuds, giving Joan's visitations a structure and stability. The news made me track down old colleagues. In some ways, I was hoping that our fragmented memories would serve to join together the realities of the space programme. In reality, I found a collection of people much like myself. Haunted, removed, curmudgeonly. Guilty about the role they had played. Still, over the years, we shared information and collated data. We postulated a link between the drive signature and Joan's own genetic profile. Meanwhile, Joan became 'Saint Joan', a viral phenomenon: to some a spectre symbolising the weirdness of everyday life in East City, to others a warning of the dangers inherent in stretching beyond the boundaries of what makes us human.

In my imagination, I would see Joan levitating about a crowd of deranged astronauts, like something from a renaissance painting of the birth of Christ. Perhaps I had become fallible to superstitions in my old age.

Four

Sleep was a shallow state for me that night, and I had the sense that I counted through all the hours before dawn. Once it was light outside, I lay in bed feeling more indolent than tired, almost lazy. I hadn't given myself time like this in the morning for as long as I had lived here. Part of the attraction of existing away from the city was the freedom to be always *occupied*, the self-reliance of exile. This morning I wanted to rest, however. I decided against disturbing Cal, not only because I thought she should sleep as long as possible, but because I couldn't yet face the interaction, that feeling of that comes when we share our private space.

Instead, I turned on a synth, retrieving the device from a cabinet beside my bed. I was a light-user of media, but I still enjoyed the synths as a way to unwind, or reflect on a particular problem. As I turned on the device, the sounds began softly, the synth picking up the pheromones evaporating from my sweat, translating them into the notes in keeping with my mood. I was surprised at how relaxed I seemed to be: the synth kept to a slow beat, chiming in occasionally with sounds. It had been a while since I'd used media in this way and it felt almost taboo. Had I an implant, the reverie would have been greater, with the synth projecting images and associations through my cerebral cortex and optic nerves. Deep within the world of the synth reverie, I recalled Cal asking the dead boy, Nathan, about Mother Ray. The music grew darker for a second, ominous and brooding. Something troubled me, but I couldn't decide what.

I must have drifted into the reverie, closing my eyes, drifting into a sense of peace and calm. When I opened my eyes, I saw Cal standing by the door.

'I'm sorry.'

I roused myself, embarrassed as though I had been discovered in some humiliating pursuit. 'It's fine. I should have been up hours ago.'

'You should come downstairs. Someone is outside. I can hear something above the house.'

She left the doorway and I pulled on some clothes. By the time I made it downstairs I could hear the sound of a hover outside. Cal met me at foot of the stairs.

'Bart. Don't tell them I'm here.'

'What?'

'I can't explain it now. But don't say that you've seen me, or that I've been staying with you.'

'Who is out there?'

'I don't know. But I don't want to know.'

'Not even if they can get you to East City?'

'I wouldn't want to be taken by them. Please don't say anything. I think it's important for us both.'

As I stepped outside, I wondered what she meant by this last remark, and what I had agreed to by inviting Cal into my home. The feeling intensified when I saw the military grade hover landing on the ground outside the wall of the house, decorated in the red ExCorp logo. The surface of the hover had been studded with malign looking weapons, and I didn't doubt that the machine could vaporise me where I stood. I let myself out, punching the code to lock the gate behind me.

Two uniformed guards left the hover first, dressed in black body armour and carrying bolt rifles, their faces obscured behind masks. A tall man followed them out: of impressive build, dressed in plainclothes, although with his combat boots and short, faux leather jacket, he retained a deliberate air of militarism.

'Good morning.' He flicked out a salute from his temple with the forefingers of one hand. 'I wondered if you'd mind answering a few questions.' From his tone, both of us knew that I didn't have a choice.

'I don't mind.'

He pointed back towards the organ farm. 'A hell of a party around there the other night.' The words assumed levity, but his eyes remained hard and essentially expressionless. 'I wondered if you'd seen anything.'

'I saw nothing during the night,' I replied. 'In the morning, I saw the smoke, but I didn't want to get involved.'

'Wise. Very wise.' He glanced back towards one of the uniformed guards by the hover. 'We probably wouldn't be having this conversation if you had got involved. Did you see anyone?'

'If you mean the cult, they've always left me alone. I don't do anything to goad them, and they leave me in peace.' I was trying to misdirect him, and it seemed that I succeeded.

He nodded, although a slight frown played through his features. 'Is that what you feel about the organ farm? They were goading the cult?'

'It's not really my business to say. They were taking a risk being out here.'

'As are you.'

'Like I said, I don't do anything to annoy them.'

'Do you sympathise with the cult?'

I laughed. 'Not really. I've reached the age where I don't really sympathise with anyone.'

He nodded his head, conceding the point. 'You're not wearing any implants, though.'

'If you must know, I spent the morning listening to a synth. Hardly the behaviour that would ingratiate me with the Luds. I know where they are and I stay out of their way.'

'So where are they?'

'You're telling me you don't know?' He didn't answer. 'They're holed up in a ruined town to the north of here. Why don't you take that hover and go and shoot up the place.'

'Maybe that's what we have planned.'

'Well, best of luck to you.' I made as if to go.

'You don't seem particularly sympathetic. A lot of people died over there. Children, most of them.'

'And I'm sorry to hear that. I like to think they understood how dangerous it could be out here, but I'm not sure that's the case. The company who hired them should take the blame.' I paused. 'And that company is probably going to want some answers from the security professionals who were hired to protect its employees. Which, I guess, is why you're here.'

The man scowled. 'I think you're getting ahead of yourself.'

'Am I? You're probably best interviewing the security personnel who were there that night, rather than bothering an old man.'

He stared at me for a second, and stepped closer. 'They're all dead. Slaughtered by the cult.'

He wore an identity badge on his jacket; I read the name. Marvell. An odd name for someone in security.

'Anyway, you're right in one way.' His tone changed to become surprisingly conciliatory. 'We do have questions to answer, and a few to ask. We're looking for the leader of the farm. Mamanea Ray. Did you see anyone fleeing that night or the day after?'

'I didn't see anyone.'

'And if you had seen anyone?'

'I don't know what you mean.'

'Would you tell me?'

'No. I wouldn't. I've already had enough of this conversation. If I wanted people to turn up at my door, I wouldn't have left East City.' The backwoods crank: that was the role I had decided to play, if indeed it was a role.

Marvell seemed reluctant to let me leave. 'What are you doing out here, if you don't mind me asking?'

'I'm just a retired scientist picking through data. Working outside the city suits me. It's good for the work, and it's good for my temperament.'

'It's an impressive looking building. Would you mind if I came inside?'

'If you wanted to come in, I don't think I could stop you.'

I thought I might be able to keep him out. I thought that by being as obstinate and difficult as possible, that I would manage to control him into being sick of interacting with me. I was wrong.

'Thanks. If you don't mind, I'll have a look around.'

He returned towards the hover and exchanged a few words with the two armed guards, then followed me through the gate. The guards spread out away from the hover, taking surveillance positions, scanning the landscape for any movement. I led Marvell inside the walls and into the house.

Cal had cleared the bedding from the floor. Marvell glanced around the living room and kitchen.

'Have you lived here long?'

'About two years.'

'It's an odd thing for you to do at your age. Give up on the city and move to the badlands. I don't know what you can have been thinking. Unless what was waiting for you in the city was worse.'

'Most people's lives don't bear scrutiny to those who step into them.'

Marvell laughed. He sounded genuinely amused. 'You do a good job of playing the wise old man. I like that. I like *you*, really. Your set up here, it's the kind of thing I'd like for myself, eventually.'

'I designed the house myself.'

This seemed to impress him. 'I like that, too. Designing your own home. Although, it's a little too distinctive. We saw it from the air, and I said to the pilot, "I have to see that place." You might regret that, one day. It's not good to be so conspicuous outside the city.'

Being away from the hover seemed to have relaxed Marvell, although probably it was another act to ingratiate himself. Even the vague threat involved in his words seemed jocular.

'It's like a return to the old days, when you bought yourself some land and created your own kingdom. I like the thought of that.' He glanced at me. 'I envy you in a way.'

'You wouldn't envy me if you knew what it was like.'

'Maybe not. But I'd like the chance to find out for myself.' He pointed to the stairs. 'And what's up there?'

'My bedroom. Bathroom.'

'Can I see?'

'Of course.'

I stayed downstairs. I breathed steadily, listening to his footsteps on the concrete; I actually felt quite calm. There were plenty of places for Cal to hide. Marvell took a while to return, longer than I had expected. Eventually, he shuffled down the steps, grinning at me as he came.

'You've made it quite comfortable.'

'Thank you. Now, if you're done with me...'

Marvell laughed. 'Have I outstayed my welcome? I'm not sure you ever answered my questions about Mamanea Ray.'

'I never knew her. She's probably dead, in any case.'

'It would be useful to know if that's true.' He smiled, although his eyes were empty. 'Besides, there were rumours that Ray had been involved in activities that went beyond her licence for the organ farm work.'

'What does that mean?'

'I have no idea.'

'Shouldn't you know that, as security head?'

'I have a large domain. It was up to my local agents to manage the day-to-day relationship. Are we speaking candidly?'

'We can do, if that would help.'

'I've been asking for more resources ever since I took over as section chief. The group based in the farm were raw, inexperienced. My local chief was a recovering dopamine addict, who wasn't really recovering. Local intelligence was thin on the ground, and Mamanea Ray was an accomplished dissembler. It was all set up to fail.'

I shrugged. 'I'm sorry to hear that. But I don't know how it affects me.'

'You say you never met Mamanea Ray? Are you sure?' His tone was engaging, as though we were old friends who had genuine experiences to share.

'Why would I?'

'I don't know. You say you're a scientist. I saw the equipment upstairs. You'd have had a lot in common with Mother Ray. Some people call her a genius. She's set herself up outside of the city in some kind of fiefdom. Like you in a way.' He let that remark hang, waiting for me to bite, but I stayed silent. He shrugged. 'The organ farm… It was run almost like one of the cults, with Mother Ray at the head. Everyone danced to her tune. I only know of rumours about the science…'

'Organ production isn't a science.' I was aware I sounded sniffy.

'Well, let's just say that Mother Ray used it as a cover. She was a company employee, but difficult to manage. Trod her own path. A lot of people were happy to let her get on with things. Rumour has it they were very excited about the kind of work she had planned.'

'What kind of work?'

Marvell shrugged. 'What the hell do I know? The way people talk about it, she was like some kind of priestess. Finding connections between things. Seeing into the future. My employers liked to think that they'd cultivated her as an asset, but we always felt that Mother Ray was calling the shots, it's just that we couldn't prove it. An outsider scientist, if you can believe in such a thing.'

Technological advances had allowed anyone to consider themselves a scientist if they so wished. Most of these amateurs were hacks and cranks, more likely to kill themselves and anyone they tested on with their body-morphing, and implant fixes. The organ farm sounded the perfect venture for a fraud like that.

'She was quite a character. Important to a few people. Some of whom, I answer to. So if you hear anything...'

For a second, we stood facing one another in the silence.

'Anyway,' Marvell said. 'I'll be on my way. We'll probably be back some time soon. It's always a lot of work, clearing up a mess like this. Perhaps I'll drop in again.'

'Oh you'd be more than welcome.'

Clearly, we'd settled into roles of mutual antipathy, and he walked quite happily back to the waiting hover.

'Remember,' Marvell called out. 'We'll be around.'

I waved him on his way, standing and watching as the hover rose into the sky. I turned around and went back inside.

The house lay quiet. I called Cal's name, but received no answer. Briefly, a moment of unreasonable panic overwhelmed me, and I imagined that Marvell had found Cal upstairs, and inflicted some form of terrible violence on her. I hurried up the stairs. With no sign of Cal in the bedroom, I climbed the ladder into the loft area, where I'd based the lab.

'Cal?' The silence answering my voice felt frozen and poised. 'Are you there?'

I heard a shuffling sound coming from the corner of the room. Cal emerged from one of the larger storage cupboards.

'Has he gone?'

I couldn't explain my relief at finding her alive. 'Yes, he's gone. I'm not really sure what he wanted.'

'Who was it?'

'A man called Marvell. Did you know him?'

She nodded. 'I saw him around the farm. He was in charge of security, the area chief. He didn't spend much time with us, though. He left it to the lower level guards.'

I laughed. 'I think he's regretting that now. He was here to cover himself. I imagine he's been put on the spot by what happened.'

She glanced across the screens, and the holoprojector winding through a set of calculations I'd run on a recent data model.

'So this is your work?'

'That's right.'

'What is it you're trying to do?'

'I'm trying to work out what happened to Joan Kaminsky.'

She nodded, but didn't add anything. The lights from the holo-model moved over her skin, as though she was dissolving into data.

'You haven't asked what Marvell wanted,' I said.

'You said he was here to cover himself.'

'He was looking for your friend, Mother Ray.'

'Is that right?' She sounded bored, abstracted, as though we were discussing strangers.

'Why do you think he wants to find her, Cal?'

'Maybe she owes the security firm money?'

'Where do you think she is?'

She shrugged. 'I don't know. Maybe she *is* dead. Or the cult have taken her back to that town up north.'

'You haven't told me much about her. I remember, you asked Nathan whether he'd seen her. That surprised me at the time.'

She scowled. 'Of course I'd ask about her. She's…'

'What is she, Cal?'

She didn't speak for a moment. 'She's important to me. She's important to us all. I was sick when I got here. A genetic condition. Mother Ray treated me for it. My sister, Elsa, was the same. Both of us had been born with a condition in our genes, and Mother Ray cured us of it. I only remember it vaguely, hardly at all. I've always felt grateful to her after that.'

Again, she seemed younger than her years. I felt suddenly guilty for interrogating a young woman who had gone through so much, who had rescued a few pathetic trophies from a dormitory in an organ farm, because they were her only possessions, because they defined her sense of self. I had pushed her too much.

'Anyway,' I said. 'I'm glad our security guard friend didn't find you. I was worried.'

'Thank you.' She looked across at me, her gaze clear. 'Bart? Why are you looking for Saint Joan?'

After everything I had asked of her, I probably deserved having to explain myself. 'I guess there are a number of reasons. She was a friend, someone I became close to. There's the mystery of it, and science has always been there to try and penetrate mystery. So that we can understand what lies around us. As a phenomenon what's happened to Joan is unique. Plenty of people are trying to work out what happened. I'm only one of them.'

'Is that it?'

'No. Most of all, it's a question of loyalty. Something happened to Joan, and I feel that we, the people I once worked for, abandoned her. I don't want to let her down. I wanted her to know that someone is here waiting for her, has been here for all of this time.'

'Did I mention that Mother Ray is interested in Saint Joan, too?'

'No. You didn't.'

'I forgot about it, really. I mean everyone has become interested in what happened to Saint Joan. But Mother Ray was more interested than most.'

'What does that mean?'

She smiled, an odd, secretive sort of expression. 'I don't know, really. A lot of what Mother Ray worked on was beyond me. She's incredibly clever. She was very excited when Saint Joan appeared that night. That's all I really know.'

This last statement was clearly a lie, but I decided not to probe any more.

We left the lab together, and walked back down through the house. We spent the evening quietly. In a back cupboard I found an old chess set, and set it up for Cal on the kitchen table, talking her through the rudiments of the game. She took to the rules quickly, and pored over the board while I cooked up a protein meal, blending it with some vegetable pulp into a casserole. The steam in the kitchen, the smell of the hot food, Cal silently, patiently making her way through the chess game… These felt like the rituals of family.

Cal seemed to relax through the meal. She even laughed when I made a joke about Marvell moving in with us. After the food, we played a few more games of chess. I was impressed at how quickly Cal had picked up the rudiments of strategy. Her pawn game, in particular, had already become advanced. 'I get it now. It's as much about the board as the pieces. About controlling the space.'

We went to bed soon after that game. It had been a tiring few days for us both, and when Cal started yawning I stood up to leave.

'You know where everything is. I'll try not to wake you when I get up. If you can't find me, I'll be in the lab.' I walked to the stairs.

'Goodnight, Bart,' Cal called after me. And then, after a pause: 'Thank you for letting me stay.'

I climbed the rest of the stairs, feeling an odd kind of contentment. Below me, Cal began to prepare a bed for the night, her movements swift and industrious.

When I awoke the next morning, she had gone.

Five

I tried not to take Cal's disappearance personally. She had been a difficult, probably damaged, young woman, who had fallen into my life out of nowhere. Our time together had been marked by a peculiar intensity, which could only mean that it was likely to end suddenly. She owed me nothing, and similarly I owed her nothing in return.

As I often did in these circumstances, I threw myself into my work. I'd collected some anomalous data from my sweep of the organ farm, and I spent the next day playing around with the data sets of the traces patterns linked to my readings of the Nordmarket. Even in a steady state, the drives created particular emission patterns and left a signature effect on the cells of anything transported through the warp. I had theorised that Joan's appearances were a manifestation of her trace genetic map refracted through the warp signature. Somehow, that trace pattern had retained a sense of integrity, allowing Joan to appear before us. The theory had prompted me to follow the main flight paths of the skuds, bringing me out to the lands beyond East City.

Every so often, I would break off to think about Cal. I wondered if she had found a way to make it to East City. I had used the word 'loyalty' about Joan. Had it been too much to expect it from Cal in return? After all, I had sheltered her, protected her, lied for her in front of Marvell. More than that, I had enjoyed our time together. I was surprised at my depth of feeling; probably I had been alone for too long. I tried to picture Cal, walking across the landscape towards East City, sleeping out in the open, hungry and cold. Even if she reached the edge of the city, on foot it would have taken a while for her to make it inside without permits, or without someone with permits to accompany her. She would end up in one of the camps on the outskirts, perhaps living there for weeks before she could persuade herself inside. It didn't make sense. Someone once told me that there was no point in pursuing a nonsensical proposition unless its possibility led to an absolute good. Of course, Cal hadn't headed back to East City. She was heading to find Mother Ray, in the Lud town to the north.

Once I realised this, I retreated from it. Unable to focus on work, I spent the afternoon out in the garden. I had been trying to cultivate a moss bed in the shade of one of the walls, and I whiled away an hour tending to the growth with some seawater I had purified from the surrounding marshland. The small, incremental growth of the moss over the earth had begun to fascinate me over the last months. I felt that in my own small way I was restoring life to this corner of the earth. As I tended to the moss, I wondered what hold Mother Ray had over Cal. From what Marvell said, the leader of the organ farm had instilled a commanding relationship with those under her charge, and her description as an outsider scientist did little to endear her to me. It was clear that Cal was putting herself in danger out of a perverse sense of obedience to Mother Ray. By late afternoon, I'd made my decision.

When Cal had disappeared, the first thing I did was to check on the hover I kept in the storage unit at the back of the garden. When I discovered it still there, with its security protocols intact, I remembered how disappointed Cal had been when I'd joked about her stealing from me. I felt guilty at the recollection. Back in the house, I prepared to leave, and pulled out the bolt pistol from its hiding place in my bedroom. I'd bought the pistol on my last trip to the Nordmarket before heading out of the city. While, in theory, the production of bolt weapons was heavily regulated, in reality any small producer with the necessary technology could print out the parts quite quickly. I fired a couple of shots in the garden, to check the thing wouldn't blow up in my hand. The pistol still worked but I felt I could hardly trust my life to it.

It had been a while since I had flown the hover, although I soon found my rhythm. Of course, flying would have been easier with an implant, wiring in the controls to the impulses of my brain, but, as with most things, the ease of implants removed what I thought of as all the human joy. Perhaps Marvell was right: perhaps I did sympathise with the cult. Up above the ground, the landscape had a peace and order to it, and I experienced a brief moment of wonder as the acceleration pushed on my sciatic nerve. The distant sea glinted in the late sunlight, the grey predictable colour of the waves looking almost beautiful, the froth catching crinkles of light. Marvell had certainly been right about my house: it did stick out in the surrounding area. I circled above the conical roof and banked northwards, passing the organ farm as I made my ascent. A fire still smouldered in the ruins. Stretched out on the ground lay bodies in their white scrubs, the sad shape of dead stars.

Something about flight had always appealed to me, probably what has appealed to people ever since they started throwing themselves off cliffs with makeshift wings. The chance to escape the limits of biology, to launch oneself into the possibilities of freedom. The sound of the engines echoed inside the cabin, a pleasing, tranquilising hum. I thought of my recent synth reverie. Some nights, unable to sleep, I would take the hover out and play a synth while I flew in the dark.

I piloted the hover carefully, flying low over the ground, plotting a course into the nav-com. The dead town occupied a stretch along the coast. It hadn't been the coast when the town was built, of course. When I'd first moved out from East City, I'd flown this area to get a sense of the geography, but also to trace any data profiles that might match the readings of Joan's appearances. At that time, I'd circled the town where the Luds had gathered, with its ruined warehouse zone, and the few glass and concrete high-rises. I'd heard on some of the meme chats that it had become something of a stronghold for the cults, but apart from a few graffiti tags, it had seemed mostly like any one of a number of dead towns on the outskirts of East City, where somehow or another people managed to make a living. To think that it represented a base for the operations, however, misunderstood the prevalence of the cults. I knew that large numbers of them lived in East City, hiding in plain sight, perhaps infiltrating the society in order to launch terrorist acts. If Marvell and his security firm really did plan to launch an offensive against this town, I couldn't see that it would accomplish much beyond the satisfaction of brutal retribution.

I saw no sign of Cal along the route. I set the tracker in the com of the hover controls to identify traces of human patterns, but nothing cropped up on the display. It was a rudimentary piece of equipment, after all, hardly efficient at certain speeds, and had mainly been installed to avoid crushing passers-by to death when landing in the city. I imagined that Cal would have hidden at the sound of the hover, anyway. After all, if she had wanted to be found, why leave in the middle of the night?

From the sat-map of the console, I could see that I was nearing the edge of the town. I'd set a doglegged course into the area, as I wanted to approach from the west, over the old warehouse district. My plan had been to fly high and come down steeply, within a close enough area to find my way under darkness into the town. People lived and worked outside East City; economies thrived. Exchanges of food and sex, exchanges of drugs and weapons: the transactions had existed as long as people had lived with one another. Anyone within East City who clung to the idea that life ended at the city walls was deluding themselves. It was easier inside the cities, more secure. But there was a class of people who survived outside of that protection, and I often wondered if the world would end up belonging to them.

It was getting late now, and the sun was setting, although the last traces of daylight still lingered in the sky. I took the hover down. Suddenly, I came under heavy bolt fire. There was no warning shot across the bows, just the blasts popping in the air beyond the craft's shell, making small explosions of blue light. One of these cracked against the exterior, sending the hover jolting beyond my control. I managed to wrestle it back on course, and took the craft down quickly, finding myself closer to the edge of the town than I would have liked. I was no expert on weapons, but I knew that the fire came from heavy bolt guns, heavier than any sidearms. I remembered how organised the Luds had been with their attack on the organ farm. Dimly, in the midst of the situation, I realised what a risk I was taking.

I killed the cabin lights as I made my way down, finding a place to land quickly, almost instinctively, on the blind side of a ruined warehouse. The bolt fire carried on behind me, and even as I set the hover down I could see the blasts in the sky. I judged that whoever was shooting was too far away, and at this point, they were surely firing in anger rather than in any hope of hitting me.

It was a hard landing but a safe one. I left the hover and inspected the damage. I had been lucky. The craft was a lightweight model, with little in the way armour. A direct hit would have caused serious damage. Apart from scorching on the tiles, the access control panel had been hit, fusing the system inside and out. None of this would affect the hover's ability to fly, but it could easily be stolen. It was unlikely that I'd need to be too concerned about theft, of course, given that had it been discovered; I imagined the Luds would burn it out.

Night fell quickly now and it was already dark in the shadows of the ruined warehouses. A patrol would surely be searching for me already. In some ways, I'd ended up in the place I'd always intended: close enough to the town to be able to reconnoitre the immediate streets, and with the hover hidden away. My plan was to get inside the town, where I could disguise myself as just another resident: no safer, but no more out of place. If that resulted in the hover being stolen or destroyed, then I could make my way back to the house on foot: a dangerous journey, perhaps, but not a difficult one. Still, there and then, I experienced a moment of despair. It was hard to decide why I'd put myself in this position: either from naivety, stupidity, carelessness, or bravado. I was too old to behave this way; perhaps I'd lost the sense of value in my life. Some skewed sense of loyalty had led me here. 'Enough to die for?' I asked aloud, and there in the ruins my voice felt a lonely thing, reedy and scared.

The warehouses had been built close beside one another, the narrow pathways between them littered with wrack. Broken brick and corrugated ceiling tiles, corroded machinery and desiccated plastic and metal, the decals and logos from long vanished corporations: the detritus of the various iterations of the town cracked and slid under my feet. Thin vines had grown up over the ground, a sickly kind of choking bindweed that I had seen often outside the city walls. Many years before there had been an infestation of an alien strain of vines, rogue flora providing an early warning that East City had become some sort of nexus of weirdness. I stuck to the walls of the buildings, hiding in the shadows, trying to control my breathing so that I could hear any traces of pursuit.

They found me faster than I'd hoped. I'd only passed a second warehouse when I heard voices coming from around the corner, the flickers of torches, and the unmistakable red strobe of laser trackers. By now, it had gone past dusk and I risked tripping over on the uneven ground, or betraying my position with a misplaced footstep. I had a torch with me, but lighting it now would give away my position. In a day of poor decisions, it seemed that I had made another.

The wall of the warehouse dipped below ground level, and I saw a short concrete staircase leading to the door to a cellar. It stood ajar. I hurried down the steps, and forced the door open, the metal grinding against the concrete. I found myself in a low ceilinged basement. Once inside, I was able to brace the door back into place, closing it quietly. I sat down on a plastic packing crate that just about held my weight. Only now that I was able to rest did I realise how tired I felt. I hoped I'd be able to hide out here for an hour or so, and then slip into the town.

At some point, I ended up on the cellar floor. I cleared a space for myself amongst the litter of concrete lumps and blistered glass. Perhaps I fell asleep. In reality, I doubt only a few moments had passed but in my stressed state that's how it seemed. I became aware of a sound outside, of footsteps on the steps, another presence beyond the door. I pulled my bolt gun from my satchel.

A voice hissed from outside. 'Bart! Is that you?'

I pulled the door open, letting Cal into the room.

Six

'I saw you land the hover. I was about to try and make my way into the town when those people started shooting at you. I should thank you, really. You made a great diversion!'

Cal seemed to delight in everything that had happened over the last few hours. From her tone, you might have imagined that we'd been involved in some convoluted game of hide and seek.

'I decided to track you down rather than heading straight into town, to make sure you were okay, and I had to avoid the group that attacked you.'

'Did you see them?'

She nodded. 'They were just a gang. I don't think they were looking out for you as such, or were acting on orders. They were laughing as they fired. I think it was just a game to them. I'm not even sure they wanted to hit you.'

'It certainly seemed that way.'

She grinned. 'I was impressed with the way you handled that hover. It was a smooth landing, considering.'

We sat together on the floor of the cellar, the plastic packet crate between us, like the chessboard back in the house. Cal seemed more relaxed, as though the threat of being caught had answered some long-held suspicion of disaster under which she intended to thrive. Every so often, we would drop our voices, at any trace of sound from outside.

'Why did you come here, Cal?'

'I think you know why I came here. Otherwise you wouldn't have worked out how to follow me.'

'Does Mother Ray mean that much?'

'I couldn't just leave her with these people. Who knows what they'll do.'

'She's probably dead already. Have you thought of that?'

'I don't think that's the case.'

'That's quite naïve, Cal.' I was aware that my voice had become patronising, needling, that I was only another old man lecturing someone younger than me.

Cal appraised me for a moment, a cool look of mild annoyance. 'I'm afraid you don't know what I know.'

'What does that mean?'

'I haven't been honest with you. We would come out here. To this town. Me and Mother Ray. She brought some of us with her when she visited the cult.'

'She *visited* here?'

'Mother Ray was trading with them. She always knew that if she wanted to run the organ farm outside the city walls, she'd need to make peace with the cult. It was clear to her that she couldn't rely on the ExCorp security detail. And so she reached out to them, and offered an alliance.'

It made sense. The assault on the organ farm had been too severe, even for a group as unpredictable as the Luds. It wasn't an ideological battle: it was a score being settled.

'What did she do, Cal?'

Cal shrugged. 'Some of it, I know about. She traded weapons from the black market. Or she acted as conduit point between some businesses in East City. The organ farm had established status, so could take deliveries out of the walls. No one could do that in the town.'

'What about the ExCorp detail? Wouldn't they have noticed?'

'Mother Ray bought them off. Whatever they wanted.' She coloured slightly. 'Some of the workers. They became involved with the security staff. Mother Ray condoned it. But not me. She wouldn't have let me get involved. It's important that you understand that. Mother Ray protected me from things like that.'

When Marvell had told me how Mother Ray had run the place, I thought he'd been exaggerating. I decided to let Cal talk, and not judge anything she said, although all my suspicions about the environment of the organ farm were being confirmed.

'Marvell must have suspected,' Cal went on. 'But Mother Ray always said that he was spread too thin. Anyway, she planned to phase out the trade with the cult.'

'What does that mean?'

'I think she was trying to control them. That was her longer term plan. She always said: 'Pay now, own later.' I wasn't sure what she meant, but I think it had something to do with Saint Joan. I don't know for sure.'

Ever since Cal had been talking, she'd assumed an almost triumphant air with me, enjoying the upper hand as she revealed everything she'd kept hidden. 'The time I told you about, when Saint Joan appeared at the organ farm, Mother Ray made it happen. I still don't know how she did it.'

'Some kind of holo, maybe?'

'You don't understand. She wasn't *faking* it. She was able to tune into Saint Joan. To make her appear, the way she appeared all those times before. All those sightings you've been researching. Only this one happened because Mother Ray caused it.'

I didn't know what to say. If true, it meant that Mother Ray had reached a level of knowledge about the Joan phenomenon that I hadn't. Cal could see my shock. She sat at the other end of the crate, toying with the piece of shattered concrete, hardly meeting my gaze.

'Where do you think she is?'

'There's a man called Gillam. He lives around here. He's influential with the cult. If Mother Ray is anywhere in this town, he'll know where she is.'

'How do you propose getting there?'

'I know the way. We went there all the time. Gillam struck all the deals on behalf of the cult. Mother Ray would take some of us along.' Cal paused, playing with a stray lock of her hair. 'I don't know why she brought me. I got the feeling...'

'What?'

She shook her head. 'Nothing. It doesn't matter.'

I decided not to probe. It was clear that Cal was starting to unpick some of her relationship with Mother Ray for herself.

'It's not too far from here,' Cal went on. 'Gillam has a house towards the centre of town.'

'I'll come with you.'

'I didn't tell you all of this to make you come, Bart.'

'I know that.' Did I? Cal had lied to me already. I wasn't sure what I understood about her anymore. I only knew that I had to meet Mother Ray, to be able to judge whether she was fraud or whether she could bring me that closer to what had happened to Joan.

We agreed to rest until before dawn, when we could head into the town under cover of darkness. We lay side by side on the floor of the cellar.

'Cal?'

'Yes?'

'How did you know it was me in the hover?'

She paused before answering. 'I recognised it from your outhouse. I went to check it out, that first night I stayed with you. I thought about stealing it. I'm sorry.'

'That's okay. I'd have done the same thing.'

We rested for a few more hours. I managed to sleep, my head resting on my satchel. When I woke up, Cal was already standing by the door. She smiled back at me.

'You were snoring. I was worried someone would hear.'

My blood sugar levels were low, and I felt unrested. I had woken in a bad mood. 'I'm sorry,' I said. 'You can't expect me to sleep properly on a cellar floor.'

'It sounded like you were sleeping pretty well to me.'

I rose slowly, my limbs feeling tense and sore. 'Are you done now?' I was aware that I was behaving peevishly, which somehow only made me feel more aggrieved.

Cal looked amused. 'You should have some water. Did you bring anything to eat?' She gestured to the bag.

I shook my head, feeling a little foolish and unprepared.

'What else do you have with you?'

'The gun. And my instruments.'

Cal smiled and shook her head. 'Bart. You're always *working*.' Her expression changed suddenly. 'Joan Kaminsky means that much to you, doesn't she?'

I didn't say anything.

'I think it's beautiful in a way. I hope that if I ever go missing, then someone will keep looking for me.'

By the time we headed outside, the sun was beginning to rise beyond the warehouse district. Cal led the way, walking hurriedly across the rubble-strewn terrain. I had grown accustomed to seeing out the dawn since I'd been living outside the city walls, one of the benefits of restless old age. Still, something about dawn in the warehouse district of this ruined old town struck me as singular. The fresh light on the tangles of metal and cracked concrete; you could almost believe that the world could be healed.

Cal led the way through an old back alley from the warehouse district, and soon we found ourselves by a ruined municipal plaza. The buildings here were of an old, toasted brickwork, most of it given up to bindweed, or crumbling in on themselves under the weight of erosion. Perhaps these had been the offices of local government, or shared spaces for the townspeople. The romantic in me imagined a library and a gallery in these spaces, filling them with books and art, the bustle of cultured people, or people who aspired to culture. The remains of benches surrounded a corroded structure which might have been a fountain. I felt caught between a sense of sadness at the loss of these communal areas, the purpose for daily interactions, and an enervated sense of peace at their rediscovery, or at least my imagined rebuilding of what they had once been.

In contrast to my pained progress, Cal moved quickly through the streets, reminding me in the way she moved of some feral mammal, its nose to the ground, driven by a secret sense or calling. Perhaps she was scared. Or perhaps she too was motivated by a different kind of longing: a reunion with Mother Ray. What hold had this unscrupulous outsider maintained over her? It was difficult to understand how someone could inspire such devotion in others.

Dismissing these thoughts, I realised that Cal was standing up ahead, waiting for me beyond the shadows of an overpass.

'Gillam lives here,' she said.

I emerged from beneath the overpass into the split surface of what had once been a major thoroughfare in the days of the old petrol highways. A white building stood nearby, three or four storeys high, with rust streaking from the pipes on the outside, a water tower on the top of the flat roof. The structure looked to have been raised in stages, erected around itself as a series of annexes and levels. The gate outside looked like a serious piece of security infrastructure.

'What's your plan, Cal?'

'I thought we should knock on the door and ask to see Gillam. What did you expect?'

'I thought it would involve a bit more subterfuge.'

Cal shrugged. She could be utterly inscrutable at times. 'Why? I know Gillam. He'll let us inside.'

'Cal, this man might have been involved with killing your friends.'

'Gillam isn't like that. You'll see. He'll talk to us and hear us out.' She turned to leave, but glanced back at me. 'Come on. It'll be fine. Trust me.'

I followed as she walked up to the front door of the house and pushed the button on the com. We waited for a few minutes, presumably as our image circulated on the screens inside the house and Gillam decided what to do. An old man walked along the street across from us, with a family of goats behind him on a stretch of twine, the smallest of the animals dressed in a tatty jumper that had been woven out of recycled plastic. The gate slid open and Cal stepped inside. I followed.

The gate slid closed behind us. We stood in a ragged courtyard, a bleached plastic bicycle lying on the warped concrete beside us. A young girl eyed us from the door of the house, a blonde girl in a soiled yellow dress. A man appeared behind her. Middle-aged and bearded, he was dressed in a white T-shirt and loose-fitting trousers. His long hair had been wound up into a scarf. His arms were decorated with geometrical tattoos, the needled kind, thin black ink on pale skin.

The man moved in front of the girl, but didn't step past the door. 'What are you doing here, Cal?'

'Hi, Gillam.'

He whispered something to the girl and she retreated from the doorway, still staring at us. 'It's not good for any of us that you're here.'

'You know why I've come.'

'I only let you in because having you standing outside my door for everyone to see would probably be more harmful. Pretty soon, people are going to notice that you two don't belong.'

I touched Cal's arm. 'He's right. We should go.'

'I need to know where she is, Gillam.'

Gillam shook his head, muttering to himself. He stepped out of the doorway and walked down towards us. His gait was slow, almost bouncy in its rhythm, at odds with his evident tension. Up close, I saw that he had a small, geometrically complex tattoo in the corner of his right eye.

'What are you doing to me, Cal? Are you trying to get us all killed?'

'They wouldn't kill you, Gillam. You're too valuable.'

He glanced at me. 'What are you to her?'

'Just a friend.'

'Then tell her she doesn't know what she's playing with.' Her turned to Cal. 'What does it take for you to get the message? How many people at the organ farm are still alive?'

'Not many.'

'Were you involved?' I asked.

Gillam scoffed at me. 'Of course not. I'm not a killer. I'm a trader. I'm a *father* most of all. I've lived in this town all my life. I'm not being forced out by anyone. I keep my head down, look after my daughter. I get along with the cult and make myself useful. Besides, do you think I want that from East City? Some of us are proud to be human.'

'I don't live in East City.'

'Good for you. Pull out the wires, and rediscover yourself, that's what I say. The cult take it too far, I know that, but fundamentally they're on the right path. I'm not bringing up my little girl to become just part of a machine.'

It was easy to see how a man like Gillam would make his home amongst the cult. For as long as people have joined together in society, we've found ways of picturing alternatives to the contracts we made with one another. We've held revolutions, forged agreements in small groups, dropped out, wandered. I had met many people like Gillam over the years, although they tended to be people of my own age, who felt out of step with the way consciousness had been absorbed into implants. We mocked the cult, called them 'Luds', but they didn't set themselves against all technology. They flew hovers, fired bolt weapons, made use of computers, even organised through some form of off-the-grid meme chats. They took against the blurring of the boundaries been technology and human. Synthetic organs. Implants. Dopamine games. Medical bots. Nano-tech. Even something as minor as a synth would be taboo for the cult, because it involved the device tapping into your physicality, using you as a source. A thing should be a thing. A person should be a person. The cult wanted to retain those borders, however doomed that might have been.

'Come on, Gillam,' Cal said. 'I know you know where she is.'

Gillam shook his head. 'The compound on the site of the old sports ground. That's where they're keeping her.'

Cal turned for the gate. 'We need to move, Bart.'

As we left, Gillam walked with us to the gate, standing in the entrance as we left. The girl had run from the house to join him, and watched as the gate slid closed.

'Best of luck,' Gillam called behind us. 'I hope you make it. If you do, don't call around here again.'

Sometimes, I wondered what would have happened if that next hour had gone the way we anticipated. I saw events the way Cal might have seen them, with a sense of confidence in her own actions, the unjustifiable self-belief of the young. Walking across town to the building by the sports ground. Scoping the outside. Freeing Mother Ray with a minimum of attention or danger. Escaping together through the town, to my hidden hover. And then, what? What did Cal imagine?

We saw the first of the hovers not long after we left Gillam's house. A black thing, high up. I thought nothing of it at the time, or rather, it registered lazily at the edge of my attention, but I was too caught up in the journey, in wondering whether some of the people we encountered (a mother in a hooded jumper escorting a brood or children, an old man sitting on a ruined cart chewing on a piece of dried protein, his eyes showing the obvious early signs of the alien bacterial infection) noticed us as not belonging.

Cal led me along a back route, through a small section of high blocks which had once seen the activity of workplaces. Hard to imagine these as sites of industry and purpose, with the glass shattered from the masonry, ground to powder many years ago. What always struck me in these ruins was the way that flora found a way of reclaiming the spaces, the lichen spreading on the corroded signs on the street corners, the patches of bindweed and vines woven around concrete. We were nearing the sports ground when we heard gunfire break out, back towards the warehouse district. Cal looked over at me, more curious than afraid.

'What is that?'

No sooner had she spoken than a hover burst over our heads. I had time to recognise the red insignia of ExCorp, as the craft banked above us, hanging in place as it turned. The engines sent dust blowing up around us. The bolt cannons began firing back towards the edge of town. The report of the weapons thudded in my chest and throat. Inside the cabin I could make out the crew, hunched and insect-like in their black masks. Small arms fire returned from some point in the street beyond us. I saw the sparks glance off the armour of the hover, doing little damage. The hover turned in the direction of the shots and began firing, the bolt guns fizzing with heat.

I pulled Cal to me, and we sprawled together back towards an open doorway into one of the ruined tower blocks. The blasts from the bolt guns sent tremors through the building, dislodging the final remains of glass from the frames. The hover banked again, and rose up in the sky, firing indiscriminately back across town.

Cal and I glanced at each other. Neither of us spoke. We had found ourselves in the middle of Marvell's revenge.

Seven

Cal's face was already grimed with dust. I assumed mine looked the same. Beyond the entrance to the office block, gunfire echoed across town, small arms and hover fire erupting seemingly from all directions. An explosion sent the ground shuddering underneath us, and in the building behind a small section of the roof fell in. Cal looked over at me, clearing her throat before speaking.

'What do we do?'

I wanted us both to head out of town as quickly as possible, of course I did. This was a far more dangerous situation than either of us could have anticipated. If I believed Cal, however, Mother Ray had found a way to establish some kind of connection to Joan, some way of decoding the phenomena. If that was right, her work was far more advanced than my own.

'How far is the sports ground?'

'About a hundred metres, beyond the plaza. If you look between those buildings ahead, you can see the stadium.'

I sized up the distance, calculating how exposed we would be in reaching it. 'Let's head there. See what happens. If we hide out from the fighting, maybe things will be a bit clearer.'

'Thank you, Bart.' Cal's expression was one of naked, almost pained, gratitude.

We waited for the gunfire to subside before leaving our hideout, scrambling out across the litter of old computer and furniture parts at the entrance. After that, we moved quickly, or as quickly as I was able. The hovers sounded in the air above the town, the drone of the engines insistent and seemingly everywhere. We ran across the plaza, keeping low to the ground. I knew that I would feel the effect of the day tomorrow, wearing at my joints and bones.

At one point, I glanced back the way we had walked from Gillam's house. A fire burned in one of the buildings, and bodies lay in the street. It occurred to me that I hadn't seen a single cult member since I'd been here, or at least anyone who visibly identified themselves as such. The people we had seen had been trying to go through the business of ordinary life. I doubted any of them had been involved in the attack on the organ farm. We were witnessing indiscriminate slaughter.

We were about halfway across the plaza when the hover appeared. I don't know if it had targeted us. I don't know if there was anything so refined as targeting involved. It flew low, suspended over our heads. A kind of timeless moment occurred. I found myself looking up at the two pilots, going about their duties with a sense of quiet purpose. I glanced down to see that Cal had disappeared. Or rather, I saw her running, then disappear, then appear again a short time later, looking back at me. And suddenly, she appeared at my side again, and took my hand in hers and pulled me. I found myself at the edge of the plaza, cowering from the bolt fire which burst over the place I'd been standing. The hover lifted off and roared down the street.

I let go of Cal's arm. 'What happened?'

'You froze. I pulled you out of there. I don't know what you were doing.'

'You disappeared. I –' I found it impossible to describe what I had seen.

She frowned. 'I don't know what you mean. Bart, there's no time. We really need to move.'

Beyond the plaza we reached the cover of a section of old buildings of red brick, long ruined and picked over, shells of habitation. The street continued into a short bridge over a canal. On the other side stood the sports ground, with the white stadium at its centre. Once upon a time I imagined that this structure had been an impressive place, drawing in thousands of people to the events inside its walls. The exterior brickwork had been sprayed with some of the recognisable tags of the cult. I could see figures scrambling outside, unpacking bolt rifles and equipment. Men and women, some of them loading up ground hovers, some of them screaming orders. Cal went to move onto the bridge, but I held her back.

'Don't. We'll be too exposed. They'll be coming this way.'

'How do you expect us to get across?'

'We'll follow the canal. There must be another way over. It'll be safer than heading in from the front.'

No sooner had I spoken than two of the ExCorp hovers appeared in the sky. They took position at a high altitude around the centre of the bridge, establishing a safe limit for their attack. I heard panicked shouts from the cult members, and shots being fired into the sky. The hovers hung there, the pilots almost taunting those on the ground. Cal and I scrambled down the bank.

'Avoid the bridge,' I called out. 'We don't want to be caught under there when they attack.'

The hovers began firing. I heard the fizzing, pulsing sound of heavy bolt weapons, the shriek of a rocket ending in an explosion on the front of the sports ground. Debris sprayed over the surface of the water. In the immediate aftermath, I heard people cry out in pain, the moaning of the wounded, but soon it was swamped by more bolt fire. The hovers began to descend, establishing a steady perimeter of fire to cover their progress. It was chilling to watch the manoeuvre, the patient, inevitable progress of the strategy.

Cal and I made it down the bank to a path beside the water. We moved along it as quickly as we could as gunfire sounded behind us. The canal curved like a moat around the sports ground, the water low and oily, tinted an unreal green colour from a particularly hardy form of algae. The two hovers had descended almost to the ground now, the sound of the bolt weapons hypnotic as they wiped out what passed for the cult's defences.

Cal and I reached a bend in the canal. Ahead, a narrow pedestrian bridge linked the bank with the outskirts of the stadium. Cal glanced back at me, almost in triumph. Behind us, the gunfire had stopped. No one now moved at the end of the bridge. Either the cult members had retreated back inside the stadium, or they were dead. One of the hovers had landed while the other maintained its position, more or less level with the stadium entrance. A figure stepped down from the access ramp of the landed hover. I recognised the faux leather coat flapping in the breeze. Marvell. He wore goggles, and brandished a bolt pistol. He fired a few shots as he advanced, flanked by two heavily armed soldiers. Even from this distance I could see the signs of a man in his element. A thought occurred to me, and I wondered why I hadn't considered it before. This wasn't some blind act of revenge by Marvell. ExCorp and Cal were here for the same reason. Marvell had come to find Mother Ray.

I stopped in my tracks. 'Cal, we need to wait a minute.'

'Why? We're nearly there.'

'Marvell. The security chief. He's just left one of the hovers.'

'So?'

'Don't you see? They're not just here to attack the town. They're here to retrieve Mother Ray.'

I could almost see the realisation hit her. She stood in front of me, open-mouthed, processing what I'd told her. 'Then it's more important that we carry on,' she said finally.

Before I could argue, Cal started running towards the pedestrian bridge. She didn't break her stride to allow me to follow. I could only call after her, hopelessly shouting her name. She didn't look back. Cal soon reached the bridge, running at an impressive speed. Something strange happened. I watched her phase out and reappear a moment later, near the end of the bridge, in the same way as she had coming across the plaza.

I felt disorientated, dizzy. I couldn't account for what I had seen, but I started to doubt I had seen it at all. Pain throbbed in my hip. My mouth felt dry; I tried to remember the last time I'd eaten. I felt defeated. More than that, I felt scared. I could cope with being an enemy to the cult, however hazardous that might have made my life outside the city walls. Marvell represented darker institutional forces, however. You might run from the cult all your life, but people like Marvell had a habit of tracking you down. Two more hovers had joined the landing party, providing air support over the stadium. Occasional bursts of gunfire sounded from inside the sports complex, but they were swiftly silenced by volleys from the hovers. The air smelled of smoke, a peculiar, ionised stench from the bolt weapons.

I don't know how long I waited. I felt exhausted, ancient. From beyond the bank behind me I could hear the sounds of gunfire echoing throughout the town, an occasional explosion. I found cover beside a large concrete drainage pipe which emerged from the bank and, seated inside, I was able to keep watch over the sport ground. I guessed that the ExCorp forces had the cult members under control. The force and resources Marvell had employed with this assault only emphasised the value his superiors had placed on Mother Ray. What had she been working on?

Fatigue let me run away with my thoughts. For the first time in the years since I'd been living outside East City, I asked myself what I'd been doing with this time. I thought of my daughter back in East City, how incredulous she had been when I decided to move out into the badlands. I had sacrificed the one genuine relationship left to me in my old age, in the name of what? ·

A hover circled low in the sky above the stadium. If I left my hiding place in the pipe, I would surely have been seen. I thought of giving myself up, surrendering. Perhaps I could have asked to be taken to Marvell. Probably I would have been executed on the spot. I tried to picture my route back through the town. Was this the moment that I had been leading up to all this time? To collapse alone in some disused drainage pipe in the middle of a warzone? After a while, I decided to explore the pipe. I crawled further along its length, lighting the way with my torch. It ran further than I expected, back underneath the plaza Cal and I had crossed, maybe far longer throughout the town. I could have used this network to find my way back to the hover on the edge of town, assuming it was still in its place. In the end, I returned to the entrance of the pipe, watching for any sign of Cal.

I must have fallen asleep at some stage: an aged man, falling into his stereotype. When I awoke, it was with a start, amazed at the sight of daylight. I heard footsteps outside, crunching the gravel of the path.

A short, overweight woman with a vast mop of curly hair appeared at the entrance to the pipe. We faced on another in silence. A moment later, Cal came into view.

Cal smiled. 'Bart. Meet Mother Ray.'

'I have to think you for your vigilance, Bart. There's something noble about you. I saw that from the first moment we met. I knew it, from the way Cal talked about you as we made our way here. Nobility. It's an under-appreciated quality these days. I find most of the people I meet are without such qualities. Without any qualities at all, really.'

Mother Ray had kept a commentary throughout our journey along the drainage system. We walked in single file, all of us slightly stooped, a position which didn't lend itself to conversation, but Mother Ray continued, undeterred. I couldn't decide whether to be irritated or intrigued by her surfeit of personality.

'I couldn't leave Cal here by herself,' I replied.

'You see.' Mother Ray said to Cal. 'A fine human being. You did well turning up on his door.'

Eventually we paused at an intersection of the drainage system and rested on a set of rusted metal machinery. Despite her endless conversation, Mother Ray was pale and I noticed her arm trembling slightly as she accepted the bottle of water when Cal passed it to her.

'How did they treat you?' I asked.

She shrugged. 'It was nice of them to extend their hospitality. We had lots to catch up on. Of course, there were a few misunderstandings we had to clear up...'

'That's one way to describe what happened at the organ farm. Cal and I went over there, looking for you.'

Mother Ray shot me a pained look. 'I didn't quite calculate how... unpredictable the cult could be. That was a mistake. I accept that.'

'You didn't pay for it though.'

She laughed, although her eyes hardened. 'The last few days haven't been easy for me, Bart. I feel like I've paid.'

'What did the cult want from you?'

'We can get into that later, if you want. From what Cal tells me, the two of us have a lot to catch up on.'

'You mean about Joan?'

Instead of answering, Mother Ray leaned back against the wall, and closed her eyes. Her face assumed an expression of indifferent repose.

'Mother Ray had already escaped when I found her.' Cal said, attempting to fill the silence. She explained how she'd found her way into the stadium by forcing open a back door. She and Mother Ray had practically collided inside the corridor.

'You're lucky that Cal found you. I think ExCorp have started this attack to extract you.'

When Mother Ray opened her eyes to look at me, I felt that it was the first time I saw her lose a semblance of control. Her lips pursed, and she looked shaken. 'I see. It almost makes me feel flattered, to be the object of such lavish attention. Almost.' She paused for a moment, seeming deep in thought. Cal retrieved the water bottle, and handed it to me.

Finally, Mother Ray spoke. 'May I ask, Bart, what is our overall goal?'

'To head into the direction of the warehouse zone, where I landed my hover. Once there, I can fly us out of here.'

Mother Ray smiled. 'Cal told me about your feat of bravado in making the landing. A fine piece of piloting, by the sound of it. A feat of dexterity and balls.'

'I was lucky to walk away alive.'

'Well, let's hope that your luck hasn't run out.' She glanced over at Cal. 'Are we confident that the hover will be waiting for us where you left it?'

I shrugged. 'I have no way of knowing that.'

'I see.' She nodded, as though in assent, although her eyes hardened. 'I'm a great believer in having options. If the hover has been compromised, what are our options?'

'We walk back across the plain.'

She grinned. 'Don't let this compact physique fool you. I'm not the most dextrous of individuals. And our friends in the cult weren't ideal hosts, let's just say. By which I mean, Bart, I don't want to walk across the plain.'

'What do you suggest?'

'Do you think we should emerge a little before the warehouse zone, to see if we can appropriate another craft?'

Cal nodded. 'I think that's a good idea.'

'There's still fighting going on. It could be dangerous.'

'Our lives our filled with danger,' Mother Ray replied. 'To breathe is to risk, after all. Particularly in a sewer.'

'I understand that –'

Mother Ray interrupted me. 'Well, do we vote or do we agree?'

I looked over at Cal, who refused to meet my gaze.

Mother Ray smiled. 'Excellent. Next exit, we rise.'

We found the nearest exit around five hundred metres from where we'd stopped: a corroded metal ladder running towards the surface. Cal went up first, leaving Mother Ray to take up the rear. 'I'd prefer to go last, if you don't mind, Bart. Call it a sense of false modesty.' Her breathing was laboured behind me. I wondered if the constant stream of speech was her way of buoying her own spirits.

Cal managed to loosen the cover of the drain, and peered through the gap to report that the streets were empty. She could hear no gunfire. We emerged, gracelessly, into the middle of an abandoned street fringed by houses and abandoned shops.

'I know this place,' Cal said, pointing westwards. 'Gillam's house is over there.'

Mother Ray stood with her hands on her sides, gasping for breath. 'Gillam. It's always good to have a local friend.'

'We've already seen him today,' I replied. 'I don't think he'll enjoy a return visit.'

'We can persuade Gillam. I imagine he'll be overjoyed to see me. Lead the way, Cal.'

Cal led us on the short walk through a series of back streets. We emerged into the same road we had walked across earlier. Behind us, the sound of gunfire echoed through the streets, but it had grown more sporadic. I checked the skyline for any sign of hovers. ExCorp would soon take to the air once they realised that Mother Ray had escaped the sports ground.

Thoughts of ExCorp vanished from my mind once we saw Gillam's house. Smoke rose from behind the walls of the white building. The water tower had been blown off the roof, and the wall had collapsed in the corner nearest to us, although the armoured door remained secure.

Cal went ahead, clambering over the rubble of the ruined wall into the forecourt of Gillam's house. When she stopped in her tracks, I knew what to expect. As I clambered up beside her, I saw Gillam lying face down on the cement. Both his legs had been blown off beneath the knee. One of his feet lay near the gate.

Mother Ray sighed. 'Poor Gillam.'

'Was it ExCorp,' Cal asked. 'Or the cult?'

'Probably a combination of the two,' Mother Ray replied. 'Not that it matters to Gillam.'

A shadow moved in the doorway. I saw Gillam's daughter emerge from inside the house. She must have been about eight years old, a slight girl who had probably been hungry all of her life. Mother Ray moved quickly to the front door, and bent down to face her.

'Hello, my darling. Don't come out any further. It's not safe.'

The way the girl looked down at the floor made it obvious she had already seen what had happened to Gillam.

'You probably remember seeing me around here, don't you?' Mother Ray continued. 'I was a friend of your father. Remember?'

The girl didn't answer, but her eyes moved to Mother Ray's face, her expression blank and uncomprehending.

'I wanted to ask you a question. My friends and I need to get away. Did your father have any kind of transport we can use? Or one of your neighbours? A ground hover? Anything that can get us away from the town.'

The girl looked down at her hands, and began twisting the fabric of her dress between her fingers.

Mother Ray persisted, her hand taking a firm hold on the girl's arm. 'Can you hear me, child? We really need to your help.'

I'd seen enough. 'Leave her alone. She's in shock. She won't be able to tell us anything.'

Mother Ray glanced back at me, and went to say something but stopped herself. 'I think you're right.' She stood up abruptly, so quickly that the girl took a step backwards towards the door. 'Come on. Let's move on.'

'What about the girl? We can't just leave her.'

Mother Ray started climbing the wrecked wall. 'I'm sure some of the neighbours will look out for her.'

'Is that really the best you can do?'

'Under the circumstances, I think it's the most pragmatic of all the options.'

'The cult probably killed her father.'

'It's not our place to judge the society in this town. They live like an extended family. Someone will look out for her.'

'I can't believe you would be so callous.'

'What would you do with her, Bart?' Mother Ray's tone had changed, becoming acidic and hostile. 'Keep her in your little laboratory? Have her run data models and tend your plants? You could take in all the strays from the whole area and build yourself a commune. Come on, Cal. Let's go.'

It took a moment for Cal to obey, and as she followed Mother Ray, she shot me a look of lingering apology. I watched the two of them clamber over the ruins of the wall, making halting progress into the street. The girl had already retreated into the house, and I was left alone with Gillam's body. From the far side of the house I retrieved a length of soiled tarpaulin and covered the corpse. I even forced myself to retrieve the severed foot, placing it under the cover of the tarpaulin. I walked to the front door, pausing at the entrance. I thought of calling for the girl, of leading her by the hand, taking her back through the town, and… what? In the end, I turned away from the house and began to climb the rubble of the wall, back out into the street.

Eight

I caught up with Cal and Mother Ray as they walked across the old petrol highway, in the direction of the warehouse zone. Cal heard me coming and turned to face me. She reached out and touched my shoulder as I got close.

'I'm glad you came back, Bart.'

Cal was unable to stop herself glancing over at Mother Ray, who was clearly in no mood to make peace.

'Leave your little friend behind, then?' she said, staring over at me with barely disguised hostility.

'I decided you were right.' I left a pause for Mother Ray to fill, but she demurred. 'Looks like you're heading to the warehouse district.'

She snorted. 'The original plan had its merits.'

'Well, you'll need me to fly the hover. Unless you want to spend time hacking the access controls.'

We continued for a while in uneasy silence. I noticed Cal glancing over at us both, probably wondering if she would need to act as arbiter in another confrontation. I had already decided to remain passive, even deferential. There was little point in rebelling against Mother Ray's authority while we were exposed in the town. It would be counter-productive and even dangerous. Beside all of that, I needed to understand what she had discovered about Joan.

We scoped out other vehicles along the way, but most of the hovers we found were too decrepit to merit stealing, while others were located off the street level, on the roofs of some of the taller properties. Mother Ray remained phlegmatic. 'We'll return if we need to, and work out a way of retrieving one of the more promising craft.' And then, perhaps in an attempt to be conciliatory. 'Bart's plan was best all along.'

Back in the warehouse district, we trod carefully in and out of the ruined buildings. The sound of activity echoed through the brickwork here and there, and I wondered if members of the cult used the place as a safe area. These signs only made it more likely that the hover had been discovered. We made plans for what we would do if so, agreeing that we would return to the basement where Cal and I had rested the night before, to wait out the remaining hours of daylight before walking across the plains under cover of darkness. All of us felt exhausted, and none of us relished the second option.

In the end, we found the hover where I had landed it. No sign of damage or any kind of interference. Mother Ray was jubilant.

'I'm sorry I doubted you, Bart,' she said. 'Our saviour and guide. Let's fly.'

It would have been better to wait for nightfall. I realised that as soon as we took flight. All of us wanted to be rid of the town, however, and for a few seconds after take-off we experienced a sense of euphoria and camaraderie. Cal sat in the seat beside me, whooping and banging her palm on the glass of the door.

My plan had always been to fly low across the plains, to avoid contact with the ExCorp hovers for as long as possible. If we'd been detected by them, they could have overtaken us easily and blown us out of the sky. I programmed in a doglegging route towards the ocean, where we could disguise our flight in some of the established commuter routes to and from East City. From there, we could make our way to my house to hide.

It didn't work out that way. Perhaps we were attacked by the Luds. Later, I would find it easier to believe that we were the victims of some zealous ExCorp foot soldiers, caught up in the bloodlust of the attack. The bolt fire rattled around us as we left the warehouse district, almost as soon as we broke cover of the buildings. A few shots burst outside the hull of the craft. I increased speed and abandoned the plan for low level flying, climbing as high as possible. I was aware of Cal screaming beside me, the report of the bolt guns outside, the whine of the hover engines as they strained to hit the ceiling at our angle of pitch. The craft shuddered and jolted, and a force knocked us from our path. I lost control of the craft. A moment of weightlessness followed, a weird vertiginous of timelessness and spacelessness, and even in the midst of this, my mind turned to Joan Kaminsky, lost in a void, a saint of the multiple, a ghost of the space-ways…

At some point I heard Mother Ray scream out in pain. I managed to regain control of the craft and pull us up from the descent. Air sucked through the hover from the rear, and I realised we'd been holed. We were lucky to still be flying; anything larger than a heavy bolt rifle would have brought us down. Mother Ray lay sprawled, her skin already grey and dull. Cal leaned over to tend to her. The back of the seat had been broken apart. The air reeked of cauterised flesh.

'She's hit,' Cal said. 'Badly. I don't know what to do.'

'We need to head to the organ farm, for the med facilities.' I remembered the young man, Nathan, how desperate he had been for us to take him to the med bay before he died at our feet.

'Do you think we can save her?'

I didn't answer. I was more concerned with how we would save ourselves. The hover listed badly, and it took a tremendous amount of effort to keep it on course. Added to that, I soon picked up two hovers on the scanner, tracking us from the town. Why they didn't overtake us I wasn't sure, although I suspected Marvell had given orders for them to shadow us until we landed.

I took the hover down to a low altitude and flew us to the organ farm as best I could. The engines struggled to compensate for the damage to the rear and the drag on the craft. Mother Ray had stabilised in the back seat, although she flickered in and out of consciousness. When I checked the scanner, I saw no sign of the trailing hovers, although I doubted we had lost them. Cal saw me scanning the air above us.

'What are you looking for?'

'Don't worry. Nothing.'

'What is it?'

'I thought I picked up a couple of blips on the scanner. But it looks like we're in the clear.'

When the organ farm appeared on the horizon, I guided us around to the blind side of the building. It was probably a pointless precaution. I imagined the ExCorp hovers had taken up position at high altitude, and would be tracing us from there. I brought the hover down as close to the compound as possible. The landing was jerky and uneven. Only when I had the craft on the ground did I realise how much the flight had taken out of me. No sleep, no food, dehydrated, a day spent running for my life. My hands were shaking, and my vision misted at the edges. I became aware of Cal pulling at my sleeve.

'Bart, I need you to stay with me.'

I waved her away. 'Okay. I'll be fine. Let's go.'

Cal and I disembarked with Mother Ray held between us. Cal directed me to a side door of the farm's compound, which led into an annex off the culture tanks. The building held an eerie, unpleasant quiet. The bodies had been removed, presumably by Marvell and ExCorp, although the grim remains of the attack remained in the bolt blasts on the walls and the blood stains on the floor. The sound of our footsteps and breathing was amplified in the empty hallways. Mother Ray shifted heavily between us. I caught a glimpse of her back. The flesh had been charred from the base of her skull down to her ribs. The force of a bolt blast would have caused significant impact damage. I didn't know if we had the capacity to save her.

Cal found a wheelchair from one of the side rooms and we lowered Mother Ray into it, still unconscious. The med-bay lay in the basement. At first, it looked like the lifts were out of order, but Cal remembered where to find the controls for the emergency generator, and brought everything back online. We headed down to the basement, the ugly emergency lighting making ghosts of us on the metal lift walls.

Mother Ray awoke as we entered the med-bay. 'You brought me home. If you can get the med-unit powered up, I can...' She blacked out again, her head lolling on her shoulders, almost comically. When she opened her eyes again, the irises were as small as pinpricks; I thought of the dots on Gillam's tattoos. 'I just wanted...' she began, but her speech dissolved into incoherence.

Cal and I undressed her in the wheelchair, pulling her clothes away as she lolled against the seat. Her body had a pale olive complexion, the fleshiness dabbed with moles. The smell of the burnt skin on her back left the sickening impression that she'd been toasted. Her breasts lolled against me as I lifted her into the unit. It struck me as odd that I'd become so intimate with this woman over such a short period of time: changing from antagonist to potential saviour. She lay on the table of the med-unit, naked and vulnerable. I covered her with a sheet. I'd been trained in med-units during my time in the space programme. The technology had moved on considerably since then, but this was an older model and I soon refreshed my memory of the controls. I managed to hook Mother Ray up to the pharma and hydration feeds, and set a scan to run across the area of the wound. She mumbled to herself as the analgesics took hold.

Cal worked diligently beside me, engaging the scans under my direction. She was silent and efficient, but I could tell she was scared.

'How are you doing?'

She shrugged. 'I've spent a lot of time in here over the years. When I was sick...' She ran a hand over Mother Ray's hair. 'How are we going to save her?'

'The first cycle of the med-unit is for diagnosis, triage and stabilisation.' I made a point of making my response factual and practical. In truth, it was entirely possible that Mother Ray would die before the diagnosis was completed. 'I've engaged the pharmacological appendages, which will help stabilise her condition. Once the diagnosis cycle has run, we can engage the bot surgery mechanisms.'

'How long will that take?'

'As long as it needs to. If we had some nano tech interfaces, things would work a lot more quickly. This is a laser appendage unit, though. We're going to have to wait until the computer has run a full cycle of Mother Ray's physiology. That can take up to an hour, unless you shortcut the process, and I wouldn't recommend that under the circumstances. The bacteria screen will also need to be completed. We're also going to have to match any organ replacements with her gene map. I'm assuming that won't be a problem?'

'Mother Ray always kept a full viscera on site, as a precaution. She always joked that she had too many enemies…'

'Not a courtesy she extended to everyone who worked here,' I said.

Cal scowled at me. Clearly, she understood that I'd been talking about Nathan, and how he'd bled to death before we had a chance to get him to the med-unit. 'Why would you talk about that now?'

'I'm sorry.' It had been a cheap remark, and utterly unproductive. I changed the subject. 'If there's any major skeletal damage, that will take longer to heal. I don't know that we have the equipment to print artificial bones.'

The readings from the scan indicated blunt trauma to the lower spine, and the kidneys, and heavy internal bleeding around the lower part of the lungs. The computer adapted to the pharma intake for blood clotting agents. I saw foreign bodies floating in the tissue around her spine, probably metal from the hover. I set about the stabilisation protocols, but I couldn't be sure that her condition was within the limits of what the med-unit could cure.

'Cal, listen to me. We're going to do all we can –'

'Bart, I –'

'Listen to me. I can't promise you that Mother Ray will survive. And we might have been traced by the ExCorp hovers.

If they arrive at any moment, I'm not sure how they'll react. For all we know, they'll pull Mother Ray out of surgery.'

'Why are you telling me this?'

'Because she has some hold over you. Something I don't really understand. But I think it has to do with your sister, and some questions you might have.'

'And?'

'I think you should ask those questions. Because you might never get another chance.'

I expected her to be upset, but she looked resigned.

'Listen.' I placed my hand on her shoulder. 'It's been a long day. I think you should rest.'

'What about Mother Ray?'

'She's stabilised for now. The surgery will be out of our hands once the computer has processed her physiology. Get out of here for an hour or so. Find somewhere to lie down.'

Before Cal left, she showed me to container unit where Mother Ray had stored her replacement viscera. I felt I was perusing some kind of unreal private museum as I glanced through the vacuum sealed bags of the various organs, a lung, a spleen, a heart all coded to her unique genetic map. I also found organs labelled for Cal and Elsa, along with other names I didn't recognise.

With Cal gone and Mother Ray unconscious, I found some protein bars in an annex off the med-bay, and drank water from a purification tank. The water was cool, almost maddeningly refreshing. The feel of it on my lips recalled a time when I was a child and my parents had taken me swimming in a mountain lake. We had stayed there for a week, seemingly removed from the problems of the dying world. The sweet taste of the water on my tongue came back to me across the years... I must have fallen asleep, and woke flailing in my seat from a dream of drowning.

Mother Ray was watching me from the med unit. 'Asleep on the job, Bart?'

'I'm sorry. It's been a long day.'

'For all of us.' Her voice came out thin and dry. 'How am I doing?'

'We've got you stabilised.'

'I don't feel well. I'll tell you that.'

'We're just waiting for the computer to analyse your physiology before starting transplant surgery. That should happen any time soon.'

'What's your instinct?'

'Honestly? It's not looking good. This is an old machine and you're carrying a lot of damage. I have you dosed up with opiates and clotting agents. It all depends of the accuracy of the machine.'

I expected some kind of wisecrack about my bedside manner, but Mother Ray only processed this information silently. 'Then I guess we'd better talk.

'If you feel strong enough.'

'I'm sure you can find some pharma blends to keep me awake. Tell me what you want to know. I'm aware you worked with Joan Kaminsky. Our Saint Joan.'

'Cal told me you were able to make Joan appear. Is that right?'

Mother Ray shook her head. Her look was almost disdainful. 'I think your problem, Bart, has been that you're too close to the phenomenon. You're still thinking of Joan Kaminsky as the person you knew.'

The remark irritated me. 'How would you suggest I think of her?'

'Isn't it obvious? As freeware.'

After she'd let the remark sink in, Mother Ray continued. 'I've been investigating the Joan Kaminsky phenomenon for the last four years, looking at it from a number of different aspects. But I have to be honest with you. I never made her appear.'

I felt a strange sense of disappointment and vindication at hearing this.

'That's not to say it isn't theoretically possible, but it's not been where I've focused. Still, there are certain patterns to the manifestations, which made it easier to predict when one might occur. I pursued it as a way of controlling the cult.'

'Why would you want to do that?'

'Because I knew that they'd infiltrated the organ farm. And because dealing with the cult outside of East City is a fact of life. And it will continue to be a fact of life long after Marvell's firework display today. If I could have assumed an element of control in the appearances, it would have held me in good standing with the Luds. Every good magician needs smoke and mirrors...' She smiled at me, weakly.

'So why were you here?'

'You've probably guessed that the sightings were recorded a long time before they became part of public record. I was set up in the organ farm to develop some practical applications of the theoretical models. It was good cover from competitors, and the two disciplines weren't exactly distinct.'

'What do you mean?'

'Let me ask you this. What do you think happened to Joan?'

'I think she became lost in the warp. That manoeuvring the craft became too much for her at a key moment and she lost integrity from the ship. Because of the unique properties of the drive, her genetic map became bonded somehow with the warp signature. That's what all the evidence would indicate.'

'You're right. And you're wrong. At least, I've come to believe you're wrong about a key part. You think it was an accident. I think it was a discovery.'

'I don't understand what you mean.'

'What if Joan didn't lose touch with the ship by accident? What if, after prolonged exposure to the warp field, she found a way to move beyond the spacecraft and manipulate the warp for herself? To move independently, free from the craft.'

'So you're saying she's not lost?'

'I don't doubt that Joan is lost, or trapped, or has hit the limits of her power. Although, I think she's probably still alive.'

'Anyway, I was set up to investigate this possibility, and to see whether the freeware represented by Joan Kaminsky could be adapted into new technology. Or maybe something beyond technology.'

'This has to do with Cal, doesn't it? And her sister?'

'Don't *judge* me, Bart.' Even in her exhausted, pitiful state, she managed to imbue that word with enormous disdain. 'I won't be judged.'

'Cal told me that she and her sister were sick when they came to the organ farm. A genetic condition. That's not true, is it?'

'One of the reasons behind setting up in the organ farm is the way that young people gravitate to them for work. And whatever you might think, I've always looked after our workers. We have all the necessary education programmes, and we health screen people when they arrive.'

'And what? If you pick up certain patterns in their genetic maps...?'

Mother Ray almost looked proud. 'Well, yes. If there are certain correlations, then I work on gene editing. Adapting the children in Saint Joan's image.'

I didn't know what to say. 'You mean Cal is... Joan?'

She shook her head. 'Cal is Cal. Although parts of her brain have been edited to resemble the brain of Joan Kaminsky. The brain that appears as a trace pattern in the warp field. I undertook the same process with her sister, Elsa, although the results weren't as encouraging.'

'What happened to Elsa?'

'My role has always been to develop the raw materials. I leave the training to other people. Elsa is at one of the partner facilities in East City.'

'And Cal? What happens to her next?'

Mother Ray shook her head. 'If you'd have seen them both when they arrived. After living on the streets of East City, grateful for food and a place to sleep. I offered her a home, and a chance to become something extraordinary.'

'You lied to her and gave her no choice. That goes against any kind of scientific ethic.'

'I wouldn't expect you to understand.' She looked genuinely affronted. 'You're only caught in my wake.'

We didn't speak much after that. It took a lot for me to process everything I'd heard. When Cal returned to the room, the sense of excitement she expressed at seeing Mother Ray ('You're awake!') might have been touching, if I hadn't found it so utterly corrupted. She poured a cup of water for Mother Ray and offered it to her lips.

'The surgery can start any minute.' I glanced between them. 'I think you two probably have a few things to talk about before we begin. Let me leave you for a while.'

Up on the ground floor, I paced alone amongst the empty culture tanks. The organ farm echoed around me. Night had fallen. I sat underneath the clear bubble dome in the main atrium, exhausted and defeated, looking up at the night sky and picturing Joan Kaminsky wandering in the space between the stars.

Nine

On my way back to the med-bay, I heard hover engines outside. I knew what to expect. Marvell and ExCorp had tracked us down. I felt almost resigned, too tired to panic. Instead, I returned to the lift and headed for the med-bay. Cal and Mother Ray turned to face me as I came into the room. Clearly, Cal had been crying.

'We need to move quickly,' I said. 'I think Marvell has arrived.'

'What does that mean?' Cal dried her eyes on her sleeve.

'We start the surgery, now.'

'And if they find her?'

'I don't know what choice we have.' I glanced over at Mother Ray. 'Are you happy with that?'

'Thank you, Bart,' Mother Ray said. 'Let's start.'

With the protocols updated, it was only a matter of initiating the bot surgery. I made the necessary preparations to the computer, and set up the anaesthetic dose in the system.

'We're ready to go,' I said.

Mother Ray nodded. 'It was good to meet you, Bart. If anything goes wrong…' The anaesthetic was already taking hold of her. She glanced between Cal and me. 'Here I go.' Her voice became a thin murmur. 'This could be my last dream.'

She faded quickly into unconsciousness. The surgery screen sealed over. As I watched the glimmer of the lasers behind the screen, my thoughts were confused. On the one hand, I found Mother Ray's behaviour monstrous, on the other I felt a sense of genuine concern that she pulled through.

Cal had turned away from the surgical table. She looked shaken, devastated.

I took her arm. 'Come on. We need to leave.'

'What if something goes wrong?'

'Then there would be nothing we can do. It's out of our hands now.' I pulled Cal to face me. 'Listen. I'll go up and stall Marvell. What did Mother Ray tell you?'

'I... I don't want to talk about it.'

'Cal, I think you need to hide. Find somewhere around here to lie low. They won't look for you, I hope. If we get separated, head for my house.' I told her the security code for the gate on my property, and instructed her to hide in the laboratory, where she had hidden before.

We walked out of the med-bay, to the emergency stairwell behind the lift chamber. Cal paused on her way through the door.

'Bart. She wanted me to give you this.'

Cal handed over a data stick. 'It's a copy of all her work on Saint Joan. The data models, everything. She said that you'd make use of it.'

I stood, almost uncomprehending as she pressed the data stick into my hand. 'I don't know what to say.'

'She wanted me to thank you for everything. You didn't need to do... any of this.'

'I know. Be safe Cal. Remember, once things have quietened down here, head for my house again.' I paused. 'I don't know what Mother Ray told you...'

'She said you'd helped us when we needed you. She was grateful for that. Don't think too badly of her, Bart. I think she's always wanted the best for me, whatever she's done.' With that, she disappeared through the door.

I rode the lift to the ground floor. The data stick lay in the pocket of my jacket, but I touched it every now and then, like some sort of totem. Up in the atrium, I could hear the ExCorp soldiers, their hard boots rapping on the floor. Underneath the bubble dome Marvell appeared, walking at the head of a small cadre of guards. He laughed when he saw me, although, as ever, his eyes were hard and dark.

'Here he is. Our friend the recluse. I can't decide if I'm surprised to find you here.'

'What do you mean?'

'We've been tracking Mother Ray across the plains. She escaped from the Lud stronghold this afternoon. I take it you know nothing about that? We lost track of her hover after a system malfunction.'

'My hover was stolen yesterday. Today, I saw it landing here at the organ farm. I came over to retrieve it and find who had taken it.'

Marvell laughed, although I could tell the plausibility of the story had knocked him off his stride.

'Do you expect me to believe that?'

'I don't really care what you believe.'

He glanced at the guards around him, as though measuring our respective levels of power. 'What did you find?'

'Nothing. There's nobody around. It seems the place is deserted.'

He gestured to the guards. 'Sweep the building from top to bottom. If you find her, bring her to me.'

'I was on my way down to the basement,' I said, deciding to trade Mother Ray to give Cal a chance to get away. 'I thought I heard something down there.'

Marvell scrutinised me, carefully, weighing up what I'd said. 'Check it out,' he said, pointing the guards in the direction of the lift.

After the guards stomped off down the corridor, Marvell said, 'Sit with me for a while.'

I followed him without a word. We walked to the foyer near the culture tanks. Up close, Marvell smelled of sweat and bolt plasma, the vague stink of death. We took a seat on one of the breakout areas from the culture tanks, a small bench beside a giant artificial cactus.

'I don't believe you, of course,' he said as we sat down.

I shrugged. 'Being naturally suspicious must come with your job. It's probably even a benefit.'

He laughed. 'That's about right.' He glanced around the room. 'You need to realise that Mother Ray is a valuable asset. It's best not to end up on the wrong side of the people who want to bring her in.'

'What has she done wrong?'

'Mother Ray thought she could empire-build. She forgot that she'd been set up here with other people's money, other people's data, other people's strategy. She's been lying to them about her work, claiming results were far less promising than they actually were. Who knows, perhaps she was going to sell the results to another bidder. Perhaps she was going into business by herself. She has a lot of questions to answer.'

'And ExCorp has been charged with settling all this.'

'Of course. We weren't here to protect the organ farm. We were here to protect the investors from Mother Ray.' He paused. 'And I don't need you to point out that we didn't do a particularly good job. Believe me, I know that.'

I laughed. 'It sounds like you've had a bad day. That puts my losing a hover into perspective.'

Any enjoyment I was experiencing in the deception, immediately soured when Marvell punched up a holo on his device.

'Have you seen this person?'

I didn't need to see the screen to know that I'd be looking at a picture of Cal. When I looked at the holo, I kept my face impassive.

'She doesn't look familiar.'

Marvell sighed. 'It's odd. We've had reports of this individual being seen around the Lud town in the company of an older man. Talking to people with links to the Luds. Even running around the cult stronghold. People said they looked like father and daughter. You wouldn't know about that?'

I didn't answer. I tested a fingertip against the spines of the cactus, discovering that they were sharp enough to draw blood. For a second, I wondered about people who felt the need to create a cactus with realistic spines. If ever there was an expression of our innate masochism when it came to the natural world, then this was it.

Perhaps I'd let my feelings of cynicism show.

'You look tired, old man,' Marvell said.

'I am tired. And I'm old. One day, you'll understand what that means.'

His gaze shifted to the kind of faraway look people assume when receiving transmissions over implants. 'I see,' he said. And then, to me: 'Come on. You need to see this.'

We headed through the atrium together. I could tell Marvell was communicating through his implant; guards moved from outside to cover the entrance behind us. I wondered if Cal had got out, or was still managing to hide herself in the compound. It seemed clear to me that she was the real prize in all of the ExCorp manoeuvres. She'd remained special to Mother Ray, as she was the most promising of the test subjects, perhaps the only one who'd shown any signs of replicating Joan's abilities. Perhaps she had already begun to manifest her powers. I remembered earlier in the day, running across the plaza and seeing the way Cal had seemed to shudder through space. At the time, I had thought it was some kind of hallucination brought on by stress. Now, I wasn't so sure.

Back down in the med-bay Marvell and I were greeted at the door by one of the security guards, a woman who had pulled the mask from her helmet. The shield still covered the table, but I could see that the bot surgery had ceased.

'She's dead,' the guard said, telling me what I already knew.

The guard went through the injuries recorded on the bot surgery interface, the trauma, the organ damage, the internal bleeding. 'It looks like she went into cardiac arrest not long after the surgery started. She hasn't been dead for long.'

As he listened to all of this, Marvell's features became even more severe. He turned to me. 'Did you know anything about this?'

'I'm as surprised as you are. Is this Mother Ray?'

He'd clearly lost patience with the course of events and my attitude of mystified innocence. 'I'm not taking any more of your lies, old man.' He gestured to the guard. 'Search him. See what he has. Search the whole place. Tear it down if you have to.'

'You can't keep me here.'

Marvell had turned towards the door, but he stopped to regard me with a look of utter violence. 'You need to understand. Out here, I make the law. I can do whatever I want.'

The security guard watched me strip. I felt there was some odd congruence, stripping as Mother Ray lay naked and dead underneath the surgery screen, as though I was being prepared for some grotesque necrophiliac ritual. The guard's expression remained blank as she searched my clothing, turning out the canvas bag onto the work surface. My bolt gun. My instruments. The empty water bottle.

'Is that everything?' she asked.

'That's everything. It's up to you if you want to look any further.'

A few moments later, I would regret that remark.

Marvell had me locked up in one of the side-rooms of the med-bay. I had retrieved my clothes, and sat on the floor in the dark. Strangely, I found it a comforting, calming experience after the confusion of the day. As I lay with my back to the door, I thought about Cal, perhaps hiding out in the building. I thought about Mother Ray, dying under the bot surgery from a heart attack. Perhaps I could have prepped the computer better, although essentially it was out of my control. I couldn't help but feel that, for all Mother Ray's duplicity and ethical transgressions, someone important had been lost.

Over the next few hours, Marvell made occasional visits to interrogate me. He threatened to take me back to East City to be prosecuted for industrial espionage. It seemed to be his main method of bargaining. I stuck to my story: the hover had been stolen from me by people unknown. When I'd seen it land at the organ farm, I'd come over to investigate. I'd only been here a matter of minutes when Marvell arrived. I had nothing to do with Mother Ray's surgery. I didn't understand what he expected to learn.

Eventually, Marvell sent one of the guards down to release me. He hadn't waited around. The guard – the same woman who had watched me strip – told me he'd flown back to East City. He had a lot of bad news to break to his superiors; I didn't envy him.

With Marvell gone, the guard seemed impatient to get rid of me. She had removed her helmet and walked around with what resembled a packet of field rations. Clearly, she'd been given the task of keeping watch over the organ farm until morning. The human factor is so rarely acknowledged in our understanding of oppression. For all the training, the dogma, the opportunities for abuses of power, sometimes the people concerned are only bored, tired and lonely, waiting to clock-off so they can head for a meal or a bed.

The guard escorted me to the ground floor level, but only watched as I made my way out of the farm complex. By the time I'd reached the atrium, she had disappeared. On my way through to the exit I stopped by the fake cactus. The data file still lay in the pot, where I'd deposited it while talking to Marvell. I folded it into my pocket, and left the building.

Back home, I waited in the garden until nightfall. I barely had the energy to stay awake, but I remained in my place in case Cal walked through my gate. In the Lud town, as we'd hid out in the basement in the warehouse district, she'd said that she hoped someone would stay watching for her if she ever disappeared. I decided that I owed her that. Eventually, I was drawn to an odd noise further down the garden. The tree, the fine sapling I had grown from a pip, was shuddering slightly at the tip. A moth had become caught on one of the twigs, a large grey moth with white speckling on its back. It thrashed around and around, unable to release itself from the twig, but when I tried to set it free, the wings disintegrated at my touch.

Ten

I never saw Cal again. I spent the next day waiting for her around the house, although in truth I had little else to do. After the day in the Lud town it felt almost strange to be returned to the banal routines of my life, and I found myself occupied by a sense of listlessness that bordered on depression. I patched up the damage on the hover, repairing it as best as I could. I tended to the garden. Eventually, I set out across the fields to the organ farm to search for Cal, although I turned back before reaching halfway. To an observer, I would have looked deranged; probably, I was talking to myself. As I headed back, I decided that I could no longer be involved with Cal and whatever might happen to her. I'd been caught up by accident in a series of schemes beyond my control.

That night I called my daughter. The vid signal was scrambled, and at first she didn't pick up, so I feared that she was still ostracising me. When she eventually answered, she looked happier than I would have expected. We talked for about an hour. She brought my grandchildren to the camera, and they played with the bioware pets, while Karla and I talked. I wondered how I'd allowed myself to become so removed from the lives I had helped create.

'It was good to see you, Bart,' Karla said at the end. 'Call again. Perhaps I'll come out some time to see you. If you think it's safe...'

If anything, the conversation left me feeling even more isolated and marooned.

I left it a few days before I looked over Mother Ray's data. Probably, I expected to find some kind of answer in what she had left me, and I told myself that answers aren't so important to science: it's the questions that drive us. When I loaded up the data sets in the laboratory, I did so almost prepared to be disappointed. And that was true, in a way. In the holo-models and visualisations, I saw that Mother Ray had been working with trace patterns and variable data that were much more highly evolved than my own. I wondered if the data I'd been working on all those years had been purposefully corrupted, and it occurred to me that my network of past colleagues had played a part in frustrating my research. Paranoia beckoned during those moments. Perhaps I was finally assuming the role of outsider scientist.

When I started the work, I did so without any real sense of urgency. If anything, I dabbled, like some of amateur. Perhaps I felt the work had been corrupted. Perhaps I saw an innate hopelessness in this project, which had left me rootless and alone. There in my laboratory in the attic of my house, something Mother Ray had said kept returning to me: I was too close to the phenomenon. It was that insinuation – that I had lost a sense of scientific rigour in my quest to find out what happened to Joan – that prompted me to return to work. Gradually, the investigation began to inspire me again. Mother Ray had said that the data had allowed her to predict when and where the manifestations would occur. It all came down to a concentration of the particles associated with the drive. I saw that she was right, and ran a model to plot the next appearance. It indicated that a visitation would occur in a week's time, at a point north of here.

When I flew out in the repaired hover that morning I felt a sense of anticipation. Years of work rested on the experiment that would take place, and, although I doubted the results would be conclusive, I felt what I can only describe as a sense of destiny. The flight path took me over the organ farm and, as I swung over the compound, I thought of everything that had happened since the day I had seen the smoke rising as I tended to the garden. The coordinates on Mother Ray's data model led me to a stretch along the coast, more or less level with the Lud town. I landed on a patch of scrub looking over the ocean.

It was a cool day, with tainted rain in the air. I could smell the sea. It oozed beyond the cliff below me, like some sort of monstrous creature, restless and diseased. We always return to water, I told myself, our origin, our birth. Perhaps, it represented our end. I set up my instruments on the ground. My plan had always been to simulate the drive signature using a specially prepared field engine, the kind we had tested endlessly in the early days of the programme. It emitted the same energy patterns involve with the warp fields, albeit on a much smaller scale.

I'd only just finished setting up my equipment when the phenomenon started.

The field began to form above me, around three or four storeys in the sky. *Saint Joan.* I recognised all the reported characteristics: the scratchy quality of the air, like the static of a corrupted holo; the sense that space had become punctured. A strange smell filled my nostrils, almost like bitter petrichor. I worked quickly with my instruments, feeding in the algorithms I'd derived from Mother Ray's data, and channelling them through the field engine. Essentially, I was opening up a doorway, puncturing the space of the phenomenon. A light began to shine at the centre of the anomaly. I saw a face forming, a body. *Joan.* I initiated the sequence from the data model. The field engine fired.

The day split into two. A bright, white light encompassed me and for a second I held up my hand in front of my eyes, and saw the bones beneath the skin, the veins inside my eyelids. When sight returned, I found myself lying on my side. I felt as though I had been spun around. I tried to stand but lost my footing, and vomited where I lay.

Gradually, I became aware of my surroundings. I was inside a forest of tall pines, the trees grown thickly together. The thin leaves were a rich dark green, almost blue. With no path through them, I had to crawl along the ground beneath the trees. The earth beneath the pines was spongy to the touch, a cushion of fallen needles browned and desiccated. I grasped onto exposed roots and sharp stones as I pulled myself along the ground. I heard rain falling, a storm erupting close overhead, a vast explosion of water, but no drops penetrated the thick cover of the trees. The journey was hard, pushing myself underneath the low hanging branches, and I needed to rest often. I lay on my back, experiencing a sensation of profound peace and safety, as though I had moved beyond harm. Nothing could come for me here. All threat had vanished. The bitter scent of the pines penetrated my skin.

I don't know how long I crawled through that dense woodland. Time lost its value and meaning. I heard the sounds of animals in the forest. Birds alighted on branches in the trees above me, birds I had only previously seen in books, sending the pine needles shaking with their weight. Foxes sniffed through the undergrowth. At one point, I lay down next to a badger for the night, or what I assumed was night. The sense of time and scale of the forest felt utterly disorientating but I felt no fear.

Eventually, I emerged into a small clearing. A house stood at the centre, a small log cabin. Light glowed from inside the window, the rich, orange light of a wood fire. As I walked to the door I felt a sense of apprehension. The door creaked inwards at my touch.

Inside, Joan sat at a small wooden table.

The wood fire burned in the corner of the room. The walls of the cabin were bare, untreated wood. Joan beckoned me to come forward. She was the same woman I had known all those years before. The riot of hair. The slender, muscular frame. She wore an orange jacket and combat trousers: her uniform from the spacecraft.

'Hello, Bart. You got old.'

'Joan.' I stepped further into the room, although my balance felt awkward. 'I don't know what to say.'

She smiled. 'It's a lot to take in.'

'What is this?'

'Think of it as a sculpture.' She gestured around us. 'I thought I'd offer somewhere pleasant for us to meet. Come and sit down.'

She gestured to a chair beside her. As I moved to join her, the walls of the cabin seemed to tilt around me. At one point, I reached out for the table, to anchor myself, but my hand passed through the wood, only for the material to tug at me. I looked over at Joan, like a child wanting encouragement.

'It's okay, Bart. It will take some time to get used to things. But we have a lot of time.'

I sat down beside her. I felt suddenly exhausted. The tiredness and confusion of all those remarkable days seemed to overwhelm me. 'I looked for you for years,' I said. Tears streamed from my eyes; I felt utterly overcome. 'I couldn't let you go.'

'Thank you.' Her grey eyes looked tired and sad, but there was an expression contained in them, beyond anything I'd ever experienced before, a distance both profound and alien. 'I wonder if you realise what you've done.'

'I needed to know where you were.'

She paused before speaking. 'I was here, Bart. I've always been here. I will always be here.' She reached out and grasped my hand. Her skin was freezing to the touch. 'And now, so will you.'

About the Author

Daniel Bennett is a writer, poet and painter. His stories have been published in *Interzone, Black Static* and *London Noir,* and he is the author of a novel, *All The Dogs.* His poetry collection, *West South North, North South East* was published in 2019 by The High Window Press. He lives with his family in East London. You can find more of his work online at https://absenceclub.com.

www.ingramcontent.com/pod-product-compliance
Lightning Source LLC
Chambersburg PA
CBHW032106170626
46808CB00008B/2960